READING LEVEL 5.1
POINT VALUE 8.0

Accelerated Reader

QUIZ NUMBER 69593

PRAISE FO_
*UNCOVE_*

"Extra entertai_ _
those who wa_ _ _ _ _ without a ghost or murder."
—*Kirkus Reviews*

"A lightweight, lively, and entertaining teen mystery-romance. Nancy Drew fans and other young mystery aficionados will be pleased."
—*Booklist*

"A great start to what looks like a continuing series."
—*School Library Journal*

"An engaging young teen mystery... A fine present for the female Harry Potter crowd."
—*Harriet's Book Reviews*

"This lightweight and enjoyable mystery will be especially appreciated by female readers and is appropriate for school and public libraries."
—*VOYA (Voice of Youth Advocates)*

MYSTERIOUS NOISES...

"Sadie? Are you there?" I called into the phone.

"Yes. It's just that they…" The knocking started again.

It stopped and I heard a buzzing, like an electronic doorbell, followed by more knocking, now quite insistent and loud. That was no next-door neighbor doing home improvement. Someone wanted in and Sadie wasn't letting them.

"Sadie, what's going on? Do you need to get the door?" I asked.

"No, no." Her voice sounded frightened. "I have to go. This isn't a good time." I heard muffled shouting in the background, then the sound of a door opening and closing.

"Wait! Tell me where you live!" I shouted into the phone.

"Barrington…," she whispered frantically. Then I heard a woman's voice—it was the voice of the Lemming Lady, I was sure of it. She was angry. "You should have let us in, you…"

Then the phone went dead.

UNCOVERING SADIE'S SECRETS

LIBBY STERNBERG

SMOOCH NEW YORK CITY

*To Hannah, my faithful helper,
critical editor, and "favorite" daughter.*

SMOOCH ®

August 2005

Published by

Dorchester Publishing Co., Inc.
200 Madison Avenue
New York, NY 10016

ISBN 0-8439-5497-3

The name "SMOOCH" and its logo are trademarks of Dorchester Publishing Co., Inc.

Printed in the United States of America.

Visit us on the web at www.smoochya.com.

Chapter One

Now before you rush to judgment and say I should have handled it differently, ask yourself what would you have done had you been in my shoes? I mean, here I was trying to hook up with a guy who was my major crush, staying on top of my schoolwork, being a good daughter, *and* having to deal with what looked to be a major, possibly life-threatening problem involving a strange new friend.

They don't cover this stuff in the "Healthy Living" classes I snooze through. Trust me, I've read the syllabus.

But I'm getting ahead of myself, which is something my sophomore English teacher, Mrs. Bernardino, says is a major problem for me. She's always circling the beginning of my reports with a fat red marker (one of these days, I'm going to buy her a slim-point gel pen in a nice muted purple), and writing things like, "Isn't this more appropriate at the end?" or "Why are you starting here?"

So, pardon me for my impatience with beginnings. I'm still learning.

The whole mess started one Saturday morning in October.

Kerrie called me at seven that morning—yes, Saturdays have a seven in the morning, too—to tell me Doug was going to meet us at the mall. (Doesn't every good story start with a trip to the mall?) With that news, I sat bolt upright in bed with no prompting from my annoying alarm clock. In fact, my heart started pounding out its own alarm and my palms got sweaty.

Kerrie is my best friend. She knows me, and she knows that deep down I think that Doug is my match, that we were destined to be together, that our paths must have crossed in some other lifetime, but to come out and admit all that will somehow make the whole thing burst like a fragile bubble.

So all I said to Kerrie was: "You woke me up to tell me *this?*"

After a little conversation in which Kerrie explained how Nicole had instant messaged her late last night with the Doug news, I padded downstairs, thinking of what I would wear now that my afternoon worldview had shifted. Passing our hall mirror, I caught sight of myself and nearly had to be taken back up on a stretcher. My shoulder-length brown hair was hanging in clumpy strings, and my face was as white as Elmer's Glue, with enchanting circles under my eyes to boot, making me look ghoulish and grumpy all at once. Heck, I *was* grumpy.

I decided to deal with the grumpy part first, by heading to the kitchen for a bowl of Frosted Flakes.

"You should eat something healthier than that!" my sister Connie said, grabbing a bottle of water from the fridge as I got out the milk. "You're fifteen, for goodness sake!" My sister is in her twenties, a slightly taller, curvier version of me, and she's a private investigator.

"For your information, that granola you scarf down by the truckload is nothing but sugar-infused cardboard. Read the label," I pointed out to her. But my gentle observation wasn't what she was in the mood to hear, so she grabbed her purse and sunglasses and headed out with a shrug of her shoulders that I interpreted as "sez who?"

In the Balducci household, we often communicate through body language. It saves a lot of time.

As I looked at the picture of Tony the Tiger grinning at me from the big box and shoveled in the crunchy sweet cereal, my grumpy mood started to lift. Almost time to get a new box, I thought as I tilted this one to pour more into my bowl. After I was done, I added it to the shopping list stuck on our refrigerator door. My mom usually does the shopping on Saturday mornings, but today she was at her boss's office downtown doing some extra work on a big case. My mom is a legal assistant in the district attorney's office. She wishes she had gone to law school and become a lawyer herself, but she's done okay for herself anyway.

Breakfast was over and I couldn't put off the other problems that faced me. First, the hair. Then, what to wear.

The best hairstyle I can manage is a casual, didn't-do-a-thing-with-it look accomplished by washing my hair before I go to bed, sleeping with the damp mess mashed into my pillow, and brushing it out in the morning so it has a sort of "windswept" appearance. This rarely fails me. It communicates a kind of cavalier disregard for my personal appearance while at the same time making me look like a younger version of Cindy Crawford who just hasn't been discovered yet.

Okay, okay. Maybe not quite.

Today, I jumped in the shower and gave it the old lather-rinse-repeat. Ten minutes later, I was sitting in my bedroom with a towel around my head swami-style while I tackled my next problem—what to wear. As I worked through these challenges, I realized it was a good thing Kerrie had awakened me so early. Looking like you don't care about how you look takes a lot of prep time.

Jeans and a T-shirt are my usual choices. But with Doug in the picture, I considered other options. It was early fall but still warm in Baltimore, so a tank top, though acceptable, was maybe too obvious. Besides, I didn't like my tank tops.

I moved from the closet to the floor, where I started to paw through a pile of clothes. Jeans and a peasant blouse? Hmmm . . . that sounded good, especially since the blouse had a hot design on it and I had worn it only once. What was it doing in this pile anyway? I pulled it out and put it aside for further consideration.

A half hour later, I had narrowed it down to the jeans and blouse versus the black T-shirt and khaki pants, but I was leaning toward the latter because that outfit would look neat but not like I was trying too hard. Besides, the black tee would look good with my new gold stud earrings, which would get lost next to the embroidery in the peasant blouse.

These hard decisions made, I went about the business of the rest of my morning, which consisted of some cleaning chores, a few phone calls to friends, a little Web surfing, and a glance at my homework assignment book just to remind myself that I was okay putting off that book report because it wasn't due until early next month.

My mother came home around noon and called up to me to make sure I was alive. My eighteen-year-old brother Tony came in shortly after that from his morning shift at the Burger Boy. Before his car keys even hit the half-table by the wall in the entrance hall, I yelled down to him.

"Don't forget, you're taking me and my friends to the mall today!"

I heard what sounded like a swear coming from his mouth, which was confirmed a second later when my mom barked from the kitchen, "Tony, watch that mouth!"

My poor mom has a lot of patience. She's been alone for a lot of years—my Dad, who was a cop, died just after I was born. She's got a lot of spunk, too, which is why she moved us back to the "old country"—from a rented house in the 'burbs to an old townhouse in a section of the city where she was raised. Which is one of the reasons Tony is taking my friends and me to the mall—so I can sort of ease into the city scene. Mom told him the night before that he had chauffeur duty.

In a few minutes, I was downstairs. Running past the mirror didn't make me panic this time. I was pretty much where I wanted to be—not too neat, not too curled, not too dressy, not too anything.

"Let's go, Tone," I called out to my brother. And we were on our way.

The mall is just north of town. It took us a good forty-five minutes to get there because first we had to pick up Kerrie in Fells Point and Nicole in Towson.

At least my family's move hadn't split up my friendships. We went to St. John's, a parochial school in the city, and people came from all over the place to attend. One of the things I like about my school (and there are very few) is the fact that you make friends with someone first, and find out where they are from and what their circumstances are later. That's because we all have to wear dorky uniforms—navy blue pants and white shirts, or a blue plaid jumper and white shirts. Wearing the same thing cuts down on a lot of clothes-envy even if it makes us feel like prison inmates most of the time.

Anyway, my friend Nicole is solid middle class. She lives in a split-level in an older neighborhood. Her father is a buyer for the county and her mother works part-time for an insurance company.

Kerrie, on the other hand, is the only child of two professionals (her father is a lawyer and her mother is a doctor) who had moved into the city as part of an urban pioneer thing. To me, her house always feels like a cross between an antiques store and a page out of an architectural magazine.

I'm not quite sure where Doug lives except I know it

is somewhere north of the city. The home neighborhood of his friend Adam—who was also meeting us at the mall—is a mystery to me, too.

After Tony dropped us off with a fond "Go get 'em, mall-rats," to which I thoughtfully responded by narrowing my eyes, we headed straight for the food court. We managed to work in our quota of giggling during the escalator ride and stair climb until we reached the food mecca, so I felt reasonably safe that we wouldn't make fools of ourselves when we came across the boys.

"Bianca!"

When I heard Doug's voice calling mine, you could have pulled out the defibrillators right then and there. He was standing by the Boardwalk Fries looking hot in an American Eagle T-shirt, olive cargo shorts, and backwards baseball cap.

Okay, so I wished he would lose the cap, but otherwise, he looked pretty cool to me. He was six feet tall, lean and muscular, with really short blondish hair, brown eyes, and a shy smile. And, from quite a distance, he had called out my name to get our attention, my name from the three that he could have chosen.

But my high spirits came crashing down when I noticed there was someone else with him and Adam. And the someone else was a girl.

Her name was Sadie, a strange name for an equally strange person. She was skinny as a rat and usually looked like she spent too much time hanging with the wrong crowd. Seriously, I'd even checked her arms for needle marks. But they were always clean. Today she wore a red tie-dye halter top and bell-bottom jeans that looked spray painted on her thighs and rear. Her blonde-in-a-bottle hair was crushed under a blue bandana and she had a gold post in her nose and about five other earrings arranged asymmetrically in each ear. Sadie had just started attending St. John's this year and hadn't made many friends.

"Look who we ran into," Adam said, smiling from ear to ear. Adam was a prankster and it was quite possible he had asked Sadie to join us just to make us all uncomfortable.

Sadie smiled a little and looked away, as if she were searching for someone. We all murmured shy *hello*s and then Kerrie, the social manager of our crowd, chirped up with a "plan." Kerrie always had plans. I think it comes from being an only child.

"Let's check out Hot Topic first. And then the Gap and then Strawberry and then maybe we can come back and have an ice cream . . ." Kerrie said.

Doug smiled at me, and I swooned.

Well, not really. I smiled back.

". . . you're welcome to join us," Kerrie was saying to Sadie.

It looked as if Sadie was about to say no when she caught sight of something, or someone, and suddenly changed attitude and answer. She shook her head vigorously and said, "Okay, let's get going! I'm kind of in a hurry!" And then she linked her arm in Doug's and started to speed out of the food court so fast I thought she was kidnapping him and I'd have to call the police.

This was not a good start to the afternoon.

Two hours later, we all sat around a table back in the food court. I sat next to Doug, who was eating a huge hot dog from Nathan's while I nibbled on a yogurt with granola sprinkled on top.

Eating in front of boys is tricky business. I've decided this is what had happened to my sister Connie. She had spent so many years pretending to like all this rabbit food stuff so that boys would think she was health-conscious and good-hearted that she had grown to like it. Heck, it could happen to me. I was open to possibilities. I took another spoonful.

Sadie sat between Kerrie and Adam, and Nicole sat on the other side of me. After our first foray into the wilds of the upper reaches of the mall, Sadie had released her grip on Doug and he had maneuvered back to walk next to me. Sadie didn't seem to mind. In fact, her urging us to get going was about the most she said during the whole time we were together. The rest of the time, she was distracted and worried, continually scanning the stores and corridors as if she were looking for someone.

"Oh, let me see what you got!" Nicole said to Kerrie, who was flipping through the pages of a bunch of paperbacks she had bought at Barnes & Noble. Kerrie pushed them over to her. "Oooh, mysteries. I love mysteries."

"I've read all of Sherlock Holmes," Kerrie said, "and a bunch of Agathie Christie."

"Murder on the Orient Express," Nicole read out loud. "That's a famous one, right?"

"Isn't that the one where . . ." I began, but Kerrie

reached over Doug and clapped her hand over my mouth.

"Don't tell me! I want to read it!" she screeched.

"Hey, Kerrie, take it easy," Doug said, and I immediately swooned again.

Well, not really. Instead, I picked up the book and started reading the back cover blurbs.

"My sister says all these detective books are a bunch of hooey," I said with sophistication dripping from my voice. "She says most of the time detectives just get boring stuff, like insurance fraud, or divorce cases, where they've got to secretly gather evidence."

"How does *she* know?" Adam asked, sipping at his Jumbo Cola.

"Her sister's a private detective," Kerrie said. Kerrie really thought this was cool and she asked about Connie all the time. "She's just getting started. She's got an office and everything, right, Bianca?"

I nodded. "Yeah. She just set up. She studied criminal justice in college, and worked with the police force in Hagerstown. My mom isn't too happy about her career choice."

"She's afraid she'll get hurt," Kerrie explained.

But that wasn't the only reason. My mother thought Connie should have gone on to study law or something like that. But Connie was something of a maverick and really wanted to strike out on her own. She told Mom that she would give the private eye stuff four years and if it didn't work out, she'd go back and apply to law school.

Tony, on the other hand, was a freshman at the University of Maryland's Baltimore County campus, studying economics, and planning on being some big financial guru when he got out. Nothing would deter that kid from his appointed course to be a multi-millionaire before he was twenty-five. It was like he was on a mission from God. He even lived at home and commuted to college in order to save money for his eventual rich destiny.

I noticed something had changed. Sadie wasn't looking around anymore. She was leaning into the table and paying attention. "Where's her office?" she asked so quietly that no one noticed at first.

"Potomac Street. Balducci and Associates," I said. "Except there aren't really any associates."

"Does she only handle those things you said— insurance . . . ?"

"No, she'll handle anything. Murder. Mayhem. Maltese Falcons," I said, proud of my ability to use alliteration in a joke. I looked at Doug. He smiled. I sighed. (Really.)

Sadie's eyes widened. "What about, uh, attempted murder?"

"You mean someone who's charged with trying to kill someone?" I asked.

"No, um, like someone being framed for killing someone."

"That's really murder. Not attempted murder," I explained, but then regretted my school-marmish tone. "But I guess, yeah, she would probably handle that. Except usually it would be a lawyer who would hire her, for the person who was being framed." Hanging around Connie had taught me a little about the business. In fact, I wouldn't mind following in her footsteps, so I was secretly hoping her venture would be such a huge success that I'd become the first of the "Associates" and Mom would be proud for me to work with my sister instead of insisting I go pre-law or pre-millionaire after I graduated from high school.

"Oh," Sadie said, and sat back, looking disappointed.

"Why? Do you know someone who's been framed?" I asked.

Sadie looked confused, then brightened. "Yes, a friend of mine. And nobody will believe her—I mean him."

I reached into my purse and pulled out a card for Balducci and Associates. "Here, give this to her, I mean him. Have him call anytime. She's got voice mail and everything and she checks it all the time." What Connie didn't know is I checked it, too. I knew her password because she had written it on the telephone instructions when she set the thing up.

Sadie took the card and looked at it, then slipped it into her jeans pocket. "Thanks," she said. She was the only one among us who had had nothing to eat or drink, *and* she hadn't purchased anything all day. I wondered if she had any money.

"Look, I was going to get a milkshake," I said standing up and abandoning my pretense of eating healthy. "My treat. Anybody want anything? How about you, Sadie?" She looked surprised, then one side of her mouth twisted up into a lopsided smile.

"No, thanks. I have to get going anyway. Getting late." She stood up. "Thanks. It's been fun. See ya." As she walked toward the door, I noticed her reaching into her pocket and fingering Connie's business card.

Tony was to pick us up at four-thirty, so it wasn't much longer before we were heading for the parking lot. Doug was still walking next to me and I wondered just what kind of touching farewell gesture he would make. An embrace, perhaps? A romantic back-bending kiss? A long look into my eyes that would be drenched with meaning? A . . .

"Well, we'll be seeing you," Doug said when we reached the floor with Hecht's department store on it. "Adam's dad is picking us up." He looked at me and shrugged his shoulders as if apologizing for the abruptness of the parting. Then he lifted his hand and it seemed to glide in slow motion as I imagined all the possibilities that this promised and how his arm would feel around my shoulders.

"Take care!" he said, gently punching me in the arm.

"Yeah, you, too," I managed to squeak out.

The two boys lumbered off, and Nicole and Kerrie and I let out an afternoon's worth of giggles and gossip in the few minutes it took us to walk to the designated pick-up spot.

"He likes you!" Kerrie squealed and I looked behind us to make sure the boys were out of earshot. Of course, with Kerrie's penetrating voice, they'd have to be in Kentucky not to overhear, but at least I didn't see them.

"Do you think he'll ask you to the Mistletoe Dance?" Nicole asked, leaning into us as we walked. "If he doesn't, you should ask him!"

"It's a junior dance, Nicky," Kerrie said. "She can't

ask him. But he can ask her. I think he'll ask you, Bianca. He might even have his driver's license by then."

"Oh, I don't know," I said, trying to sound disinterested. "Maybe he'll ask Sadie."

Nicole and Kerrie both burst out laughing simultaneously, then got a case of the guilts and stopped just as abruptly. "That was weird running into her," Nicole said.

"Yeah. I didn't quite picture her as the mall type," Kerrie added.

"Neither did I. She seems more the downtown type, if you know what I mean," I said. They all nodded and we all imagined Sadie wandering into incense-laden bookstores and little boutiques that sold tie-dye shirts and Indian skirts.

"Where's she live anyway?" Nicole asked.

"Don't know. She kind of hangs by herself," Kerrie said.

"Maybe we should try to get to know her better," I said as we walked through the doors of the mall to the dark parking lot. I looked around. No Tony. He was late, as usual. "She looks like she could use a friend."

"Or a probation officer," Nicole said.

"Nicky!" Kerrie cried and rapped her on the arm.

"Just kidding."

In the distance, I saw Tony's blue Civic wending its way through the rows of cars. In a few seconds, he was at the curb, and we all piled in. He said nothing to us and we chatted among ourselves during the ride back to our homes.

After we dropped off Nicole and Kerrie, the silent

treatment continued. The radio was broken in his car, so we couldn't even listen to that. As we headed east toward home, I stared out the window at the gray landscape. The sky was overcast and the air was beginning to cool.

Doug had called my name and punched me in the arm. Not bad for an afternoon's work.

Chapter Two

That night, my family ate at Cara Mia's in Little Italy, a restaurant my great-aunt Rosa Molvone owns.

Aunt Rosa is a big lady who always reminds me of a small tug boat the way she nudges and pushes everybody into doing what she wants. And, she's a little on the chunky side, to put it charitably.

Although I know she's my mother's mother's sister, I can never tell if she is pushing fifty or ninety. Her hair, always pulled back in a tight bun on the crown of her head, is coal black from the henna rinse she regularly uses on it.

She used to own the restaurant with her husband, my great-uncle Cesare, but he passed away two years ago. Everybody says Aunt Rosa has been a different person since then, and from the way they nod their heads when they say it, I take it that widowhood suits her.

"The shrimp scampi is good tonight," she said, hovering over our family's table. "Good shrimp. As big as clams. And the lasagna is fresh. Just made it this afternoon." Her hawk-like eyes caught sight of the empty bread basket on our table. In a flash, her hospitable mood changed to haughty anger as she scooped it up, turned to a waiter, and spit out something in Italian, which I assume meant something like "Get more bread here, you bumbling son of a one-eyed witch."

My mother, who knows a little Italian, grimaced. "Whatever you recommend sounds good, Aunt Rosa," she said, and Rosa left to place our unarticulated orders in the kitchen.

Once a month we went through this ritual, coming to Cara Mia's, pretending to look at the menus, and letting Aunt Rosa (or Uncle Cesare before her) pick out what we would eat. When I was a kid, it didn't matter much to me since I couldn't understand the menu anyway. But now that I was older, I wouldn't have minded selecting something for myself, like a veal dish or surf and turf from the "American Food" column.

The first time I'd uttered that wish to my mom, however, she'd reacted as if I had told her I was joining up with the Heaven's Gate fellows. "Surf and turf at Aunt Rosa's? She'd never speak to us again!"

If Tony and Connie were ever told the same thing, I don't know. They just put their menus down with a little eye-rolling and waited for their dinners. The refilled bread basket soon appeared, placed on the table by a dark-skinned, dark-haired young man who gave Connie the once-over as he walked away.

"Why don't you ask him out?" Tony said, reaching for a slice.

"Shut up, jerk," my sister softly replied.

17

"Do any business today?" I asked her and she looked at me like I was crazy.

"Business? You mean work?" Connie asked.

"Yeah. Work. Like find any missing treasure or locate some kidnapped heiress," I said.

Connie's mouth turned up on one side. "I think you've been watching too many old movies."

"No, she was at the mall today with those hoodlum friends of hers," Tony interjected, his mouth stuffed with bread.

"Don't talk with your mouth full," my mother said.

Tony swallowed. "I had to take her, too. And I had a lot of stuff to do."

"You mean like multi-tasking?" I asked. To Tony, multi-tasking was watching TV and napping at the same time.

"Like getting started on a history paper," he said in a "so-there" voice.

"It's always such a pleasure to spend this quality time with you all," my mother sighed, and we settled down.

"Seriously, Con, did a girl by the name of Sadie Sinclair call you?" I asked.

"No. No one by that name," Connie said. "Why?"

"Nothing, I guess. She's a new girl from school and we ran into her at the mall. When she found out you're a PI, she started asking some questions and I ended up giving her your card."

"Questions about what?"

"About being framed for—a crime she didn't commit," I said, deliberately leaving out the fact that Sadie had specifically mentioned "murder" as the crime. Didn't think that would play real well with my mother.

18

Connie paused before answering. "No, no Sadie called asking about that."

"Well, if she did, how would you go about helping her?" I asked. Just then, my Aunt Rosa returned with two plates that she put on the table with a flourish. One held an antipasto selection and the other was a steaming hot platter of stuffed mushrooms.

"Mmm, those look great," my mother said, smiling at Aunt Rosa.

"Yum, crabmeat," Connie said tasting one. Tony reached for two.

"Your dinners will be out soon. Enjoy," Aunt Rosa said.

"Connie, you didn't answer my question," I said.

Connie kept eating, taking some of the salami and ham and provolone from the antipasto plate. Her health-food regimen went on pause whenever we came to Cara Mia's.

"Well, it's a tough question," she said slowly. "It depends. I mean, has the crime been reported to the police, and if so, what do they have? That's where I'd start."

"What kind of trouble is your friend in?" my mother asked.

"None. And she's not really my friend," I answered. "Just some new girl."

Two hours later, I was lying on my bed wondering why I thought I could eat that last cannolli when I had already wolfed down appetizers, lasagna, salad, and bread.

It was a typical Saturday night. Connie was in her room and Tony was downstairs watching television.

Mom was reading in the living room. Sometimes Tony or Connie went out on dates or with friends, but it wasn't unusual for us all to be hunkered down in our own little worlds.

I thought about calling Kerrie to debrief her on the mall visit and scope out what she thought of the possibility of Doug asking me to the Mistletoe Dance and what I would wear if he did. But I decided to get a Coke first because Coke always calms my stomach. I wandered downstairs to the kitchen in the back of the house, past my mother in the living room.

In the darkened kitchen, I could hear Tony's television booming away down in his basement room as he flipped from WWF showdowns to C-Span to AMC and back through the dial.

Our house was an old row home where the kitchen had originally been in the basement. Renovations had moved the kitchen to the first floor, within easy reach of the dining room, so everything in the kitchen was new, including the wiring. My mom had put the family computer in that room on a desk against the side wall, where it could easily be plugged into a dedicated line that wouldn't fizzle out if the circuits shorted, and could easily be connected to the telephone line, too. I glanced over it as a screen saver played out a scene of a lawn mower blazing through rapidly growing grass.

Coke in hand, I decided to sit down at the computer and do a little investigating of my own before calling Kerrie.

"I'm getting online," I called out to my mother and anyone else who would hear. I sat down at the small desk and pointed and clicked my way into cyberland, first answering a couple of emails from school chums, including one from Kerrie that would save me a phone call.

"tried to call you but no answer," she wrote. "marsha called. she said doug is definitely interested in you, asked about you last week at some debating club thing. remember that rose velvet dress at lerner's? that would look good for the mistletoe dance . . ."

I wrote her a quick note back, thanking her for her intelligence report, reporting to her that Sadie hadn't called Connie about the "attempted murder," I ate too much at dinner, and was now going to look up where Doug lived. I sent it off and a few seconds later got an instant message back, heralded by a wind-chime noise.

"Turn off the sound, hon," my mother called from the living room. So I pushed the off button and watched the screen as Kerrie weighed in again.

"sadie is spooky. marsha says she talks like she's from somewhere else. doug lives in towson, near nicole but don't know exactly where . . ."

"How come you never told me?" I IMed back.

"you never asked," came the answer a second later. "how do you know sadie didn't call connie?"

"I asked her," I wrote Kerrie. Then we went back to gossiping about school, complaining about our teachers, and bemoaning the fact that we didn't have any study halls together. An hour later, Connie came into the kitchen and glanced at me as she went to the fridge for water.

"You still on? You're tying up the phone!" she said.

"We've got voice mail. Besides, I'll be off soon," I

said and waited for her to leave before signing off with Kerrie and wandering into an Internet search engine. I punched in the name "Sadie Sinclair" and waited. Most of the places I searched didn't turn up anything, but I did get a few interesting hits for some artist out in California named Sadie Mauvais Sinclair.

Just for fun, I went to a few of those articles, one of which had a photo, but the artist looked nothing at all like our Sadie Sinclair. She was a Tahitian woman who specialized in "neo-primitive paintings with an island theme."

I dutifully checked the voice mail after logging off and there wasn't a single call for my family of forgotten souls. But before I put down the receiver, I decided to check the voice mail again, not our voice mail but Connie's office. After all, I did know the password.

I punched in the numbers and waited. "You have two new messages," the electronic voice said. I checked them both, careful not to do anything to them, but neither was from Sadie. One was a telephone solicitor, the other a call from a client about rescheduling a meeting. I was about to hang up when I decided to listen to the "saved" messages as well. There were three of those.

The first two were run-of-the-mill calls about ongoing jobs. Then, bingo, I heard her voice.

"Hi," she said tentatively. "I'd like to talk with Constance Balducci . . . a friend recommended you . . . for a friend of mine . . . Anyway, I'll call back. I guess you're not in on Saturdays. My name is . . . Bobbie McCormack . . ."

Bobbie McCormack? I hit the replay button and listened again. That was no Bobbie McCormack. It was

Sadie's voice. This was getting too weird. First, she asks about private eyes to help "a friend" with a frame-up for murder, then she uses a fake name? I hung up the phone and meandered back upstairs, trying to figure out what to do with this information. Information is power, I always say, so it's best to think it through before spilling all you know.

I sat in my room awhile, hugging a pillow to my chest while I listened to a couple CDs. Then, I walked down the hall and rapped on Connie's door.

"Yeah?" she called out.

"It's me."

A few seconds later, she came to the door and opened it, letting me in.

"What?" she asked. She had on her robe, and a towel was wrapped around her head. She had slathered some cream on her face that smelled like cucumbers and looked like guacamole. New Age chant-like music was coming from her CD player, and a bottle of nail polish was open on her dresser. After she let me in, she went back to polishing her toenails a deep red color, sitting in an old rocking chair by the window. I sat on the edge of the bed. "What can I do you for?" she asked.

"You know, I forgot to mention this. That friend who I gave your card to—her name was Sadie but she said the friend that needed help was Bobbie McCormack. Did Bobbie McCormack call you yet?"

I saw her pause for maybe a nanosecond as she decided whether to share any information with me. Then, she finished polishing her right toe nails, capped the bottle, and spread her feet in front of her as they dried.

"Bianca, part of being a private investigator is keeping people's business private."

"Come on, Connie. If she called and left a message, you haven't even had a chance to talk to her. So, it's not really private yet." Strange reasoning but enough to do the job.

"Okay," she said. "Yeah. Some gal named Bobbie called today. But she didn't leave a number. She just said she'd call back."

What a sleuth I was! I just found out something— that I already knew! Sherlock Holmes, watch out.

"Well, I didn't tell you but she said this friend was being framed for murder," I said.

Connie leaned back in her chair and got serious. "Murder? That's nothing to fool around with. And that would be in the police reports, in the papers. That's not something that goes unnoticed."

"I thought it was kind of odd myself."

"What's your friend like? The one who said her friend is being framed?" Connie asked.

"She's new to school this year. And she's different. Keeps to herself mostly. Really skinny. Nobody knows much about her."

"Maybe you should get to know her," Connie said, and I perked up immediately. Wow. Connie was asking me to help on a case.

"Yeah. That would help. I could find out stuff."

Connie frowned. "No, you doofus. I meant maybe you should get to know her because she's new and it would be nice for somebody to reach out and make her feel at home."

"Oh. Yeah. I was getting to that," I said. In the dis-

24

tance, the phone rang. I ran down the hall to grab the extension in my room before Tony could pick it up.

"Bianca! I'm so glad I got you," Kerrie said breathlessly on the end of the line. "Nickie just called and told me the most incredible news . . ."

"What? What?"

"She said she saw Sadie going over to Doug's house."

My heart sank. I sat down on the bed and pretended not to care, and listened while Kerrie told me the whole gruesome tale.

Chapter Three

By the time Monday morning rolled around, I had imagined a hundred different scenarios for why Sadie Sinclair, Woman of Mystery, would be visiting Douglas Patterson, My Own True Love, on a Saturday night.

The Saturday night after the afternoon in which he had punched me in the shoulder and called out my name.

Unfortunately, none of the scenarios was really good for me. They ranged from torrid romantic liaison to secret science project cloning the school's star basketball player.

So, I wasn't in such a great mood when I showed up at St. John's at eighty-thirty a.m. in my perky plaid jumper and white Peter Pan blouse. As I rolled the dial on my locker lock, Kerrie came up to me. We had already exchanged numerous calls and email messages throughout the weekend filled with speculation on the reason for the Sadie-Doug rendezvous, and she had promised me she would find out for sure by Monday morning.

"Hi," I said, trying to keep myself from grabbing her, shaking her by the shoulders and screaming out—*What did you discover? Tell me, for goodness sake! Tell me!*

"So what's up?" I asked.

"I tried Marsha twice last night and couldn't get her," she said, trying not to look me in the eye. Marsha was a junior who was friends with Adam. She and Kerrie had been on Student Council together the year before and still talked from time to time. Marsha was very popular and knew everything about everybody. But you had to be careful talking to her because she would reveal what she heard about you as easily as she would reveal what she heard about others. It was just as well if Kerrie hadn't been able to get hold of her. Talking to her twice in one weekend about Doug and me would surely switch the rumor mill into overdrive.

"That's okay," I said, grabbing my morning books and putting my lunch bag in my locker. "I'll figure out what's going on. It's not like Doug and I are going out, anyway." Did Kerrie roll her eyes when I said that? I couldn't tell.

The morning bell rang and we went to our respective home rooms. It would be lunchtime before we were able to catch up with each other again.

But I was true to my word. I spent the morning trying to "figure out what was going on." Whenever I passed Doug in the hall, he smiled at me, a big open smile even in front of his friends.

On a scale of one to ten, with one being "don't want to be seen dead with her" and ten being "setting a date with the minister," those smiles qualified

27

as a solid five. Maybe even a five-point-five, depending on how you looked at it. Meanwhile, I didn't see him send one grin Sadie's way. Of course, I couldn't see them together all morning.

That changed at lunchtime. The cafeteria was in the basement of the old school building. Shock-therapy bright with white tiled floor and white walls and fluorescent lighting, it was as noisy as the inside of a drum at the end of the William Tell Overture. The sound of one hundred kids chattering and clinking silverware and ripping open paper bags was enough to put any rock concert to shame.

I headed for my usual table, near the door that led to the auditorium hallway, where Kerrie and Nicole were waiting for me. Carmen Smith was with them and so was Hilary Stone. Carmen was a black girl from Liberty Heights, and Hilary was from somewhere near the Pennsylvania border. She was absent a lot when the weather was bad. We all hung together in a loose group. We liked to think of ourselves as the "anti-clique clique" because, although we stuck together as shoulders-to-cry-on when things got tough, we didn't always eat lunch or hang out together as a lockstep unit. In other words, we played well with others.

"Hilary wants to know if we want to be in the school play," Kerrie said, rushing past me to get in line to buy her lunch. She always bought her lunch while I always brown-bagged it.

"Try-outs are this afternoon," Hilary said, coming over to me. "And I thought we could be like moral support for each other." *Translation:* Hilary wanted really badly to try out but she was afraid to do it on her own.

"What's the play?" I asked. "And what do you have to do?" I plopped my lunch on the table and started to open my bag. Peanut butter on whole wheat (thanks to Connie), apple, granola bar, bottled water. I started eating.

"It's a musical," Carmen volunteered. She was already eating what looked like a ham sandwich with tomato and cheese and lettuce. Wow, it looked good. *The Mikado.*"

"Gilbert and Sullivan," Nicole said, nodding her head. "Don't you have to sing something in the tryout?"

"Yeah, but anything you want. Nothing special," Hilary said. I suspected she had an audition piece she'd been working on for months. Hilary was really bitten by the stage bug. She even looked like an aspiring actress, with auburn hair in a pixie cut framing perfect features that (against school rules) she highlighted each day with mascara and eyeliner and a touch of blush. She was so skillful with the makeup brush that she never got caught. "Mrs. Williston said we should try to get as many people to try out as we can. She needs choristers. And especially guys."

Hmmm. Guys. That was a good excuse for revving up the old conversation machine with Doug. Might be worth a try. I scanned the room looking for him. On Mondays and Wednesdays, he had lunch at the same time I did.

"You could sing just a Christmas carol or something, or even the National Anthem or a verse from one of the songs we sing in chorus," Hilary pleaded. "If we don't get enough people, we can't do the show."

"Look, I don't mind coming to give moral support, but I can't commit to a rehearsal schedule," Carmen said. "Williston will have you there every night the week before the play, and I promised my mother I'd be home more this year after doing band all last year." Carmen had deliberately cleared her schedule so she could have time for Advanced Placement courses. She was taking AP History this year and counting on going into AP Physics next year. She wanted to be a rocket scientist.

I noticed Doug entering the room from the opposite side. He was laughing and talking with Adam and some other guys I didn't know well.

"All right," I said with a shade too much enthusiasm. "Come on, Hilary, let's round up some men for Mrs. Williston. I'm game!" I grabbed her arm and pulled her with me down the length of the lunch room, passing a puzzled-looking Kerrie juggling a food-laden tray. "It's showtime!" I said to her by way of explanation as we passed.

Spontaneity is a good thing. If it hadn't been for the idea of roping in some guys to try out for the show, I never would have screwed up the courage to talk with Doug that day, or probably any day after it.

When we made it to his table, he looked up and smiled at me again. A huge neon sign flashing *"five, five, five"* in my brain nearly blinded me and sent me reeling, but Hilary was on a tear so she covered for me easily.

"Mrs. Williston really needs guys to try out for *The*

Mikado," she said and I swore I saw her bat her eyelashes. Hilary was one of the few students who actually looked good in the uniform. Heck, she looked like a model for the uniform. "If she doesn't get enough, she doesn't want to do it. She doesn't want to use a lot of girls dressed up as guys."

The guys all started looking down and around—in fact, everywhere but at Hilary—and it was clear that this idea was going over like the proverbial lead balloon. But then she added some deal-sweeteners. "There'll be a huge cast party at the end of the show, and Mrs. Williston is getting passes out of first bloc classes for everybody on the day after the show, plus she said she might need to schedule some rehearsals during the day and she'd make sure it was all right with the other teachers."

It was as if little bells were ringing in each guy's head. Ping! No first bloc Algebra? Sounds good. Ping! I could get out of old Rathbone's History of Civilization? Sounds good. Ping! Cast party with music and girls and . . . Heh-heh.

I was nearly deafened by all that mental pinging.

One of the boys spoke up. "What time are the auditions?" he asked nonchalantly.

"Three. Right after school. And she promised it wouldn't interfere with any athletic schedule."

"Are you going to try out, Bianca?" Doug asked me. He talked to me! Yippee skippy! I did a little dance.

Well, not really. I smiled.

"Yeah. I thought I'd give it a shot," I said. "Maybe get in the chorus." I had no desire to be a leading lady. Too much pressure. Although I wasn't quite sure

31

what I wanted to be, I had ruled out Star of Stage and Screen as well as rocket scientist.

"Come on, Doug, Bill, Ryan," Hilary pleaded. "It'll be fun."

"Okay. Maybe I'll try," Doug said at last, and I thought it was significant that he was the first to speak after I had volunteered my own intentions to try out. I could see a causal relationship between the two.

"Three o'clock!" Hilary said, triumphant.

As we turned to go back to our lunches, I caught sight of Sadie. She was coming into the lunchroom late and she looked as if she had been crying. That had to mean she was detained by a teacher or called into the office for something.

In addition to her binder and books, she held a note in her hand. It must have been an office visit, with the principal or assistant principal or guidance counselor. Her nose ring and earrings were gone, and she had pulled her hair back into a stubby ponytail at the nape of her neck. When she saw me, she smiled and I remembered Connie's admonition to make friends with her. Given that I was on an information-hunt, it seemed like a good idea.

"Sadie! Come on down to our table," I said to her, and she accepted the invitation with the same enthusiasm as a lost traveler in the desert taking an offered glass of water. As she passed Doug's table, he called out a cheery hello and I forced myself not to think of where it fell on the scale.

If Kerrie was surprised when I showed up at our table with Sadie in tow, she didn't show it. She just scooted her books out of the way so Sadie could sit down, and went back to finishing her cream of chicken soup.

"I better hurry," Sadie said to us before heading off to the food line. We only had fifteen minutes of our lunch period left. As soon as she took off, I looked longingly at the books she had left behind. There, smack on top, was the piece of paper she had been carrying, folded over. I couldn't just unfold it and read it. That would be outright nosiness.

So I accidentally bumped her books close to the edge while moving my stuff around to make room, and before I knew it, her things were on the floor.

"Bianca, you're such an oaf!" Kerrie chided me.

"I'll get it, don't worry," I said, bending over to pick up the fallen items. Quickly, before raising my head above the table, I scanned the note. It wasn't a detention or disciplinary letter at all. It was a short typed note from the principal, Mrs. Weston, to "Amy Sinclair" notifying her that her daughter Sadie was showing exceptional progress in math and computer skills and that her teachers were recommending she be advanced to the next level.

"We have been unable to reach you to schedule an appointment to discuss this matter, so would you please call us at your earliest convenience," the letter ended. Hardly the stuff of moping looks and tear-stained cheeks.

I stacked the books neatly on top of the table, being careful to place the note in its folded position exactly where I had found it.

A few moments later, Sadie returned with a tray full of food. She had opted for the hot lunch, a full meal of roasted chicken breast, mashed potatoes, lima beans, applesauce, a brownie, and both a milk and a bottle of iced tea. It looked like she was stocking up for a rainy day. As soon as Sadie sat down, Carmen turned to her and wasted no time finding out what we all wanted to know.

"You're from California, aren't you?" she asked brightly. "Dale Levy said you were."

"Uh-huh, that's right. San Jose," Sadie said between bites. She ate like it was her first hot meal in a week.

"Why'd you move east?" Carmen continued. It was amazing how much information you could get through direct questions.

"My mother has some family here. A cousin," Sadie said. "And she wanted to be closer . . ."

Carmen nodded. "Must have been hard leaving California."

"Not really," Sadie said, finishing up the mashed potatoes and opening up the brownie wrapper. "I like it here."

"How about your friends? Wasn't it tough to leave? I mean, after freshman year?" Nicole asked.

This was great. My friends were doing the interrogating and all I had to do was sit back, listen, and finish my peanut butter sandwich.

"No. This school is much nicer. And . . . I can write to my friends . . . or call," she said, but it was such a half-hearted claim that I doubted she had spoken with even one old friend since moving to Maryland.

I was hoping that Nicole or Carmen or Kerrie would continue with questions about Sadie's family, her old school, and what she was doing at Doug's last night, but the effervescent Hilary chimed in with her requests for try-outs for the show.

"Everybody's going to do it," she said breathlessly. Hilary only knew how to speak breathlessly. She didn't have any other way of communicating. "You ought to come. It would be a great way to meet people."

Sadie smiled, and it was a genuine smile, which made me feel both good and guilty at the same time. I was, after all, human, and I knew it must be tough to try to fit in at a new school all the way across the country from what had been familiar. So, my heart went out to her and wanted to make her feel wanted. But on the other hand, I had only invited her to eat with us because I wanted information, so I also felt two-faced. To make up for my moral deficiencies, I decided to be as hospitable as Hilary had been and then some.

"Yes, you should come," I said with conviction. "I've heard you sing in chorus and you've got a great voice."

Sadie beamed at that compliment and her face took on the same look she had sported when I first invited her to sit with us—a sort of desperate joyfulness. "Thanks," she said shyly.

At three o'clock, we were all sitting in rows in the auditorium, snickering and giggling and kicking at each other's seats. Doug had come in with some of his friends and Kerrie was skillful enough to get up at just that moment and move us all down a few seats so that he could sit next to me. Which he did. I needed oxygen.

Well, not really. But I did blush with nervousness as his elbow glanced against mine on the armrest between us. He smiled at me again, and asked me if I had ever been in a show before.

"Just in grade school," I said.

And I gave a stellar performance, too, I thought, as one of the shepherds in the Christmas tableau. Of course, it would have been even better if I hadn't snagged Joseph's fake beard with my crook and he hadn't fallen over the creche trying to reach for it, but then again Mary didn't have to let out a mild expletive when he stepped on her sore toe and pulled down the set when he grabbed for something to keep his balance. It wasn't my fault he thought the painted canvas stable was steady enough to support him.

But I kept this nostalgic memory to myself.

"I was in *On the Town* my sophomore year," Doug said in a low voice that sent a shiver up my spine. "It was fun."

The room hushed as Mrs. Williston called out the first name from the roster of those of us who had signed up. A timid-looking freshman with bright red hair went up to the stage after giving some music to old Mr. Baker, the accompanist. Then she started to belt out "Tomorrow" from *Annie* and was actually pretty good, but we all hated that song, and were super glad when it was over. Mrs. Williston had the girl read a few lines, then called out the next name, and the next and the next.

Most of the kids were, like us, new recruits with nothing special planned. Mrs. Williston asked such auditioners to sing the first verse of the school song, which got kind of embarrassing because a lot of us didn't really have it committed to memory. She gave up on that after a few tries and just asked for the first verse of "Silent Night" from then on.

Hilary, of course, was the star of the auditions, singing Yum-Yum's aria with perfect poise. When even Mrs. Williston burst into applause, there was no doubt she had the part. When my turn came, my knees were knocking so hard I was afraid they'd throw Mr. Baker's rhythm off, but I managed to chirp out a verse of the Christmas carol without completely embarrassing myself. I'd get picked for chorus for sure. I could tell from Mrs. Williston's "thank you" she clearly wanted me to know I was welcome in her troupe, just not too welcome.

Almost everyone in our crowd had auditioned when Sadie came into the auditorium and found us. She scooted down the row of seats in front of us so she could turn and talk to us.

"I almost forgot about this," she explained. "I was in the library." Then she turned to Doug. "Hi, Doug," she said.

To reclaim the center of the universe, I started talking, or whispering rather, since people were still auditioning. A senior was on stage bleating out "Send in the Clowns."

"Sadie's from California. Did you know that?" I asked, hoping Doug didn't know. If he did, he didn't let on. "The weather must have been great there."

"It was okay," she whispered.

"I bet you saw a lot of movie stars all the time," I said. Boy, was that a sophisticated observation.

"Not really," Sadie said. "I lived in kind of an artsy area but no movie stars or anything like that."

Artsy? My Internet search came to mind.

"You wouldn't be related to Sadie Mauvais Sinclair, would you?" I asked, trying to sound intellectual. I turned to Doug to explain. "She's a Tahitian-born artist who deals in neo-primitive island themes."

I hadn't expected Sadie to recognize the artist's name or even to give a rat's petootie about her. I had merely thrown it in to show off, but I didn't pick up any admiring glances from Doug, just a blank stare.

But Sadie's face—it was as if she had seen a ghost. Her face drained of the little color it had and her smile faded immediately. Her eyes widened with fear and her brows furrowed.

"Sadie Sinclair," Mrs. Williston called, and Sadie turned and went to the stage like a condemned woman walking to the gallows.

Chapter Four

When Sadie mounted the steps to the stage, I felt a simultaneous surge of unease and anger. Unease because, obviously, something I said had upset her. Her face was whiter than parchment and her bouncy mood had completely vanished. She now walked slump-shouldered to center stage, awaiting the moment when Williston would give her the signal to begin.

But I was also angry. Why did Sadie have to step on every move I made with Doug? Even without Marsha broadcasting it all over the school, it had to be obvious to Sadie that Doug was—well, special to me. And I was angry for feeling uneasy, too. I hadn't done anything wrong, right? I crossed my arms over my chest and glowered at the chair in front of me.

"Ah, yes. Sadie." Mrs. Williston's reedy voice cut through the auditorium, which had grown strangely silent. It occurred to me that Sadie Sinclair was viewed as an odd bird by everybody in the school, someone who kept to herself and tried not to stand out. I straightened and leaned forward.

"She looks nervous," I whispered to Doug.

"Aw, she'll be okay," he said.

But she didn't look okay. She managed to squeak out a "yes, ma'am" so low that Williston had to ask her to repeat it. Staring at Sadie over her little half-glasses, Williston sighed with such bravado that even the balcony seats could pick up her little bit of stage business.

"My dear, please try to project. Now, what would you like to sing?"

At first, Sadie said nothing. She looked at Williston, then at the stairs on the other side of the stage as if contemplating a break for the door. Then her eyes lit on me, and by golly I couldn't help myself. I gave her a big, go-get-'em grin and then—I couldn't believe I was actually doing this—a thumbs-up sign with my right hand. A wan smile flickered at the corners of Sadie's mouth.

"Uh . . . I can sing a folk song. . . ."

"Okay, dear. What is it? Do you need accompaniment?" Mrs. Williston was tired. Sadie was the last to audition.

"No . . . I can do it a capella . . ."

A capella? Where had this girl learned music terminology?

"The Streets of Laredo," Sadie announced. Then she stood stock still, fixed her eyes on some unknown point above the balcony and, like a meadowlark, proceeded to warble the old cowboy song about death and sadness. She had a sweet pure voice, just the kind that was made for folk songs.

The auditorium had been built before microphones were commonplace, so its acoustics provided a natural amplification that enhanced a good singer's voice. Sadie's carried to the last slat of the last seat of the last row. When she was finished, we all applauded. It seemed to come from us spontaneously, as if we weren't in control of our hands. At least that's the way I felt as I smacked my hands together. Or maybe I was making up for the guilt.

Mrs. Williston, too, was impressed. She stood up and asked Sadie to come talk with her privately.

"What a nice voice," Hilary murmured from down the row. Call me crazy, but I don't think Hilary was all that happy about Sadie's nice voice. Until this moment, Yum-Yum was hers for the taking.

With no one left to audition, we all stood getting ready to leave. Sadie continued talking with Mrs. Williston while the rest of us aimlessly tried to make conversation.

"I was thinking of having a Halloween party," Kerrie chirped. This was news to me. "Costumes and all. My folks said it was okay."

Out of the corner of my eye, I caught sight of Sadie swiftly walking up the aisle. Instead of joining us, her new friends, she rushed out of the auditorium with the same red-faced look she'd worn coming into the cafeteria earlier. Despite my desire to stand alarmingly close to Doug, I broke away and ran after her.

"Be right back," I murmured to my circle.

I caught up with Sadie outside the big double doors to this wing of the school. She stood shivering in the cold, her arms wrapped over each other. Her face was mottled from unshed tears.

"Sadie!" I called over, trying to sound casual. "You were terrific!"

She smiled shyly. "Thanks."

"We're talking about a Halloween party," I said lamely. Then again, blurting out "What's the matter with you?" didn't seem like the right thing to say either. "Kerrie's house."

"Oh . . ."

"I'm sure she'll invite you." After I told her to, that is. "Thanks."

"Do you want to go inside? We were just kind of hanging out." To make a liar out of me, Doug and Kerrie and Hilary and Nicole came out the door just then. Doug handed me my jacket and backpack, a small gesture of kindness that nearly made me hysterical with joy. But I controlled my emotions.

"There you are!" Kerrie said to me, then turned to Sadie. "What a voice. You're full of surprises, Sadie."

"I was just telling Sadie about your party," I said.

"Well, yeah, I have to pick a date. It'll be a weekend."

"Make it a Saturday," Doug chimed in. "I have to work on Friday nights." Did he look at me when he said this? Was this a message intended for me? I took it that way, mentally filing it away under "Why Doug Won't Call on Friday Nights."

"A costume party, right, Kerrie?" I asked, trying to divert attention away from Sadie, who still looked troubled.

"Uh-huh," said Kerrie, smiling at me and nodding in Doug's direction. I think she was trying to tell me that this was my chance to have some soulful conversation with the guy. "I gotta get going, Bianca. Give me a call," Kerrie said, running off towards the parking lot in back of the school. She was getting a ride home with a senior who would leave without her if she was too late.

Hilary and Nicole also said hasty good-byes and went off to catch their rides and buses. That left an awkward trio of me, Doug, and Sadie.

Doug shuffled a little, looked at me, then at Sadie, and my amazing new mind-reading powers led me to believe he was wondering if I was going to ditch her so we could talk. I'm ashamed to admit that, if given half the chance, I would have thrown Sadie into the bushes then. But something happened that threw us all for a loop.

A large black car, expensive-looking with tinted windows, cruised past the front of school, slowing to a stop near the end of a long wide walkway that connects the auditorium doors and the street. Sadie saw the car first and her eyes widened. Her hands clenched at her sides as her white face flushed with heart-pounding fear.

Doug, being a guy, was oblivious to this. His eyes were focused elsewhere. "Cool car. That your ride, Sadie?"

She said nothing, but rushed into the school instead, leaving Doug and me on the steps with the mystery car just a few yards away. When Sadie disappeared, I figured the car would move on. But it didn't. It stayed put.

A few seconds later, the passenger door opened and a tall, sallow redhead dressed all in black—black leather pants, black leather jacket, black tee—got out. As she sauntered towards us, the window rolled down and a man's voice shouted at her to get a move on.

Without turning around, she picked up her pace,

teetering forward on high-heeled boots that made her look like a bowling pin about to tip over any second. As she got closer, I could see that she was heavily made up with black eyeliner rimming reddened eyes, brownish lipstick, and eyebrows that didn't match her hair color.

"Can I help you?" I asked, and she looked at me like I had just spit at her.

"Yeah, I guess. That girl . . ." Her voice was nasal and high-pitched.

"Sadie?"

The woman smiled. Or rather, she smirked. "Sadie," she repeated. "Yeah. Sadie. Where'd she go?"

Doug stepped forward. "Why do you want to know?"

My hero.

"Uh . . .'cause . . . I . . . I have to talk with her. . . ."

"Are you her mother?" Doug asked. Her mother? I nearly slapped my forehead with my hand. If this woman was Sadie's mother, I was Jennifer Lopez.

"Uh . . . yeah . . . yeah, that's right. I'm her mother and I need to talk with her," the woman said, but before I could cackle uproariously at this obvious untruth, Doug chimed in.

"Oh, well, she's probably gone back into the auditorium to get her things. Here, I'll show you." He turned to open the door. My *chivalrous*—but slightly dense—hero.

I jumped between him and the door. "That's okay, Doug. Look, I'll show her. I want to talk with Sadie anyway. Thanks. I'll talk to you soon, okay?"

Doug shrugged and looked a little disappointed, which was okay by me. Maybe he had been counting on another pal-like punch in the arm followed by a cheery farewell. Better to keep him wanting.

As he walked off, I turned and opened the door for "Sadie's mom," making small talk along the way.

"So, how do you like Maryland, Mrs. . . ." I paused just a breath, hoping she'd chime in with "Sinclair." When she didn't, I continued my snooping, using the techniques I had learned at lunch earlier that day— direct interrogation. "I'm sorry . . . I don't know your name."

So many kids had divorced parents these days, you could never be sure if their mother's last name was still the same as theirs, right?

"Uh . . . Sadie . . . Just call me Mrs. Sadie." She giggled nervously, and her thin heels clacked on the tile foyer to the auditorium. No one was around. I led her to the doors, first glancing in through the tiny slit between them. Sadie was gone. I shoved open the doors with a flourish.

"Oh dear, she appears to have left already. Let's go look for her locker," I said in my "most-helpful-parochial-school-student" voice.

I started walking at a brisk pace towards the cafeteria. It was highly unlikely that Sadie would be in there, but there was something about this "Mrs. Sadie" (how lame could she get!) that made me want to keep her away from her "daughter" as long as possible. As we came near the other end of the lunch room, I caught sight of Sadie through the slender glass window that ran the length of the doors. Her eyes widened and I saw her take in her breath. With an imperceptible nod of my head, I communicated— Balducci style—to "get the heck out of here." Getting the message, Sadie turned back toward the locker hall.

"So, what brought you to Maryland?" I asked conversationally as we ploughed through the doors to the next foyer. Avoiding the locker hall straight ahead, I turned right and headed up the stairs to the offices and first floor classrooms. She followed, lemming-like (if you can imagine a lemming in black leather and high-heeled boots).

"Huh? Nothing. Just travel. We like to travel."

At the first landing, I made a decision to bypass the first floor and head on up to the third. This lady wasn't used to exercise and was huffing and puffing before we even reached the next level. Keep her in a weakened state—that was the ticket.

"It must have been hard to leave . . ." I was going to say "California," but stopped myself and substituted "New York" instead. "Such an exciting city. Baltimore must seem like a small town in comparison."

"Yeah, well . . ." she said between huge gulps for air as we headed up the third flight. "It's not—so—bad—once—you get—used—to it." She sounded like the oxygen had been sucked out of the room.

The third floor was dark and I headed to an even dimmer hallway that led to the art rooms. Outside the rooms were several rows of unused lockers. The teachers stored art supplies in them. I had a slight hunch "Mrs. Sadie" wouldn't notice that these lockers had no locks on them.

"Oh dear," I said with mock despair. "She's gone. She must have left. She hates to miss her bus. I'm sure you'll catch up with her."

The woman had nearly doubled over trying to catch

her breath again. But her agony gave me a chance to go to a tall arched window that overlooked the back of the school. In the distance, beyond the softball field and track, I could see Sadie rushing off campus. She would be safe now.

"Catch up where?" Straightening, the woman's demeanor changed. The artificial smile was gone and any semblance of concern for her "daughter" was now replaced by anger. "Where did she go?"

"Home—home, of course," I sputtered. All of a sudden I wished I hadn't led her up to this secluded floor. We were completely alone. The janitors wouldn't come up this far to clean for hours. And Mrs. Sadie was beginning to look like Mrs. Sinister.

"Well, where the hell is that, Miss Smartypants?" she hissed at me. It didn't seem the right moment to point out that, as Sadie's "mother," she should know where home was.

"Camden," I improvised. "Down by the ballpark."

She advanced on me, sticking her hand in her jacket. I didn't want to know what was in the pocket. I started walking quickly to the stairs again.

"I'm sorry. I assumed she lived with you. I guess she lives with her dad. . . ." I started skipping down the steps, flying over them so fast I risked tripping. "I have to go myself, didn't realize it was so late. I'm sure you'll find her," I called over my shoulder as I ran.

As I reached the first floor, I felt a painful yank at my hair and nearly fell. She had somehow gained on me, and now pulled me up short, bending my neck back as she tore at my roots.

"Listen, sister, I need to find her and quick. Where is she?"

The searing sensation of having my hair ripped out by the roots made tears come to my eyes. My heart was thudding so loud in my chest I was sure she could hear it, and I kept wondering two things: when would her pal in the black car come looking for her, and had he taken the same course in "Manners for Thugs" that she had obviously aced?

"I don't know," I managed to squeak out. "I honestly don't know. Nobody knows much about Sadie. I thought I heard her mention Camden. I think that's where she lives . . ."

She pulled her hand out of her pocket, and, to my horror, she not only was holding a knife, but its thin edge was coming close to my arm.

"When you see her," the woman snarled at me, "tell her that her mother wants to talk to her real bad." With a heart-stopping movement, she grabbed my backpack and, with the knife, slashed through its strap. It fell off my arm, thudding to the floor. Just as quickly, she let go of my hair and walked out the front door. As soon as I saw her go, I ran to the office to call my brother. I wanted a ride home. This was definitely not a day for the bus!

That night at dinner, I could hardly hold my fork steady. I was still trembling from my afternoon encounter. I was so distracted that I let Tony grouse uninterrupted for ten minutes about having to pick me up at school that afternoon. After telling him to stop complaining, my mother told me I'd had a phone call. "Forgot to tell you," she said. "It was on the voice mail when I got home. Must have come in when Tony was picking you up." She reached for the salad and put some on her plate after eyeing the huge uneaten pile of it on Tony's. "Sadie, it sounded like."

"Did she leave a number?" I asked with sudden interest.

"No, she said she'd call later. Is she a new friend? I haven't heard you mention her."

"Just another low-life she hangs with," Tony sneered, but Connie kicked him under the table. Sometimes Connie was all right. I could tell from her silence at the table that she was in one of her "can't wait to move into my apartment" moods where quality family time wouldn't be a big factor.

"Yeah, she's a friend of Kerrie and me," I said and finished off my baked chicken and Rice-a-Roni as fast as I could. "May I be excused?"

"All right. But you're doing dishes tonight."

My shoulders sagged. "Con, can I switch with . . ."

"Not on your life. I've got a serious date with Lexis-Nexis tonight," she said.

Ouch. Double bad news. Not only would she not do the dishes for me. She was going to tie up the phone doing Internet research.

"Okay, okay," I said and headed for the hallway. "Just let me make a quick call." I grabbed the broken end of my backpack strap and climbed the stairs to my room two steps at a time, first taking the cordless phone off the hall table as I went by.

"What did you do to your backpack?" my mother called after me. She missed nothing.

"It just broke. That's all."

"That's an L.L. Bean," I heard her murmuring as I reached my room.

Before the backpack hit the floor, I had already dialed *69. A ring, then a nasal electronic voice came on. "The number of your last incoming call was . . ." I grabbed a piece of paper and pencil stub in a frantic effort to catch the number, only to hear the phone number of the school pay phone pop up. It was my call to Tony, not Sadie's call to me. Disgusted, I hung up and quickly dialed voice mail, feeding in my sister's office number and password. A few run-of-the-mill messages and a hang-up. Why did I have the strong feeling the hang-up was Sadie?

One last try—I dialed Kerrie's number. But before it could ring through, I heard the telltale clicks of my sister using the phone line to log on to the Internet. I hung up and silently cursed my continuing bad luck.

Chapter Five

"You know, we should get one of those dedicated Internet server lines—the ones that connect to your cable television or something," I complained a few minutes later to Connie, who was flipping through Web pages with lightning speed. The dishwasher was humming along and I was scraping rice bits out of a sauce pan in the sink.

I was jittery to get online myself for some cyber companionship. Ever since my encounter with Lemming Lady that afternoon, I'd been on edge. I mean, someone slicing through your backpack is nothing to sneeze at. Even though I consider myself to be pretty unflappable (okay, okay, except maybe around Doug), the blade in Lemming Lady's hand was enough to put the fear of God into me.

Only problem was I had no one to talk to about my fears. Mom was scared enough for us already. First off, she's, well, a mom. So naturally, she's protective of her brood. But given the fact that my father was killed in the line of duty, she's probably a little more nervous about us than normal. Talking to Connie or Tony about the incident was out of the question. I mean, they're my siblings.

"I'm getting a dedicated line at my office," Connie said, bringing me back to reality and out of the worry wormhole I had been sucked into.

"Well, we could use one here, too. What if one of us had an emergency and we called home and the phone line was tied up all night?"

Connie gave me a look that said "the weather must be nice on the Planet Moron," then echoed her thought with: "You have my cell phone number. Plus, in case you haven't noticed, we're all home now. If you have an emergency, you can just walk over here and tell me."

I ignored her sarcasm and finished my scrubbing, dumping the clean saucepan into the dish drainer, drying my hands on a towel, and walking over to the computer.

"What are you looking for?" I asked, standing behind her as she scrolled through a page heavy with type.

"Just some information," she said noncommittally, then looked at me and shrugged as if giving up the fight. "I have a client who suspects one of his employees is cheating on him."

"Oh, and he hired you to prove it?"

"Not exactly. He just wants to get rid of the guy with no fuss, no lawyers digging into his accounts. So I'm just giving the boss enough information to show the employee it's best to leave of his own accord."

The material Connie was perusing, I noticed, was an article on "How to Dismiss a Problem Employee" from an old *Business Month* magazine. So much for glamorous private eye work.

You've got mail, chirped the computer, and Connie minimized the article to open her email.

"This is great," she said, scanning the note. "This will do it!" As she printed out the note, I read it. All it told her was the social security number of one "Herb Bolvane."

"How does that 'do it?' " I asked. "It's just a number."

Connie pointed to the first three digits in the nine-digit number. "It's much more, my dear. It tells me his place of birth, or at least where he lived the first years of his life. My Mr. Bolvane is a liar."

At my perplexed look, she continued her lesson. "See the first three numbers?" She pointed to the screen where Mr. Bolvane's first three digits read 034. "You can tell from those where the card was issued. Mr. Bolvane's was issued in Massachusetts—010 through 034 are Massachusetts numbers. But he claimed to his employer he was a lifelong Marylander." She turned around and started typing a response.

"How do you know he's a liar? Maybe his mother got him his card when he was a baby and they were only in Massachusetts a little while," I said, pleased to think of it.

"Uh-uh. In Mr. Bolvane's case, the second two numbers are 00. No Social Security numbers were issued with that as a group number. It's a fake number. He's a liar all right."

As she typed her note, I left her alone, marveling at the wonders of the private investigator universe and hoping she'd be off the phone line soon in case

Sadie was trying to call me. I went upstairs to do my homework.

It turned out to be a disappointing evening. Connie stayed online for another hour. When I tried to reach Kerrie, she was out buying some school supplies with her dad, which meant IMing her wouldn't do a bit of good, and Sadie either didn't call or didn't bother to leave a message when she did.

I went to bed feeling lonely, grumpy, and nervous, which I discovered was a surefire way to keep sleep at bay.

The next morning, I was determined to talk to Sadie alone. In spite of my initial misgivings about the girl, I was beginning to feel like she was in some kind of big trouble and might need some help.

Maybe I was motivated by guilt for originally making fun of her. Or maybe it was because of Lemming Lady. If she scared the bejeebies out of me, she must surely do the same for Sadie.

Whatever the reason, I now felt like a "Woman with a Mission" and fixated on finding out as much as I could about Sadie's situation. This goal-oriented approach was a great fear-reducer. It energized me and made me feel in control of the situation.

Despite arriving at school early, I couldn't find Sadie. She wasn't at her locker, and Kerrie, Nicole, Carmen, even Hilary (whom I was sure would be tracking her new rival's every movement) didn't know where she was.

I shuddered. What if the leather-clad Lemming Lady had actually found Sadie? I fingered my slashed backpack strap and pushed the horrid thought from my mind.

"Did Doug ask you out?" Kerrie whispered as we made our way to first period. "You two looked awfully cozy after school. That's why I left in a hurry. So you could have more time together."

"No, he didn't," I told her. "He was real nice, though. But we got interrupted." I wanted to tell her more, but the bell sounded, and there was no more time for small talk.

This set the stage for the rest of a day, when there would be no time to catch up on gossip. Normally, I'm a pretty good student. My favorite class is Creative Writing, where Jolanda Murphy and I exchange Fan Fiction stories we write about our favorite television shows. But today, not even that class was enough to keep me focused.

I was even late for lunch because I had an algebra quiz that took me longer than usual to finish in my distracted state.

By the time I got to my friends' table in the caf, I barely had enough time to wolf down my peanut butter sandwich and listen to Kerrie's cheerful chatter about her Halloween party.

"Everybody *must* wear costumes," she announced emphatically. "No civvies allowed. That way, everybody will get in the spirit. I hate it when you go to a Halloween party and only a couple people come dressed up."

I had the impression that Kerrie had been one of those odd ducks more than once.

"What will *you* be?" I asked her, trying to get in the

spirit even though what I really wanted to talk about was my encounter of the day before.

"I don't know. Maybe Mata Hari."

Mata Hari, famous spy. That was no off-the-cuff response. She probably had been planning the costume for months.

"What about you, Bianca?" Kerrie asked. "You could wear something really hot to get Doug's attention."

"I'm not good at that stuff, Kerr."

"I'll help you! Come over Saturday. We can throw something together. We've got tons of old clothes."

"Maybe we can invite Sadie, too," I said, the thought coming out of my mouth at the same time it arrived in my brain. Kerrie looked a little perplexed at the suggestion but rose to the moment.

"Sure, sure, whatever. Where is she today anyway?" She looked around the lunch room.

"I haven't seen her. And I need to talk to her," I said. I wanted to tell Kerrie about the mysterious car and lady but not in front of Hilary, or anybody else for that matter. "I'll call you tonight," I continued conspiratorially. I think Kerrie got my message. She gave me a knowing look.

The day ended as it began—with me looking this way and that for Sadie, trying to figure things out with the small pieces of information I had, and trying to look for opportunities to spill it all to Kerrie.

On every front, I was frustrated. No Sadie, no solutions, and no moments with my best friend who had to leave early for a dentist's appointment and wasn't even around for some quality bus-stop time.

This was a Doug-free Day as well, a day when our

schedules were completely out of sync. So I didn't see my boyfriend-in-waiting once, not even after school because he had taken off with friends to catch a school football game. A total bust, I thought, as I stood at the curb waiting for a bus. I would go home, try to reach Kerrie later, do my homework, think some more about this situation, maybe even toss around a few costume ideas.

The bus roared up to the curb and a few of us St. John's kids sashayed on. I moved to the back and sat alone by a window.

Just as we lurched forward into traffic, I looked down and saw—the black car! It was following me.

Panic gripped at my throat, choking me. My breathing came fast. I had to get off this bus. But where, I wondered? Normally, I got off two blocks from home and walked the rest of the way. Nobody would be home yet. Mom was still at work. Tony would be on campus until late tonight. Connie was probably at her office. Connie's office. It was not far from home. Think, Bianca, think! Was there a bus stop near there? Could I stay on the bus until then?

I had to suppress a strong urge to run up to the driver and tell him to step on it and lose the black car. Instead, I slumped down in my seat, hoping the Lemming Lady and her invisible sidekick wouldn't see me.

Of course they saw me, I thought in annoyance. That's why they were there. They were looking for Sadie and they knew I knew something about her. Except I didn't know where she lived. Or even her phone number. I felt like making a sign and hanging it in the window. *Futile Mission,* it would read. *I know nothing!*

A consoling thought came to mind. If they were pursuing me, it had to be because they didn't know where Sadie was either. That meant she was okay and the Backpack Slasher/Lemming Lady had not gotten to her. Yet.

I looked out the window again. The car was still there, deliberately missing opportunities to pass the bus and make better time. They were definitely following me. How long had they waited outside the school? What else did they know about me?

The bus turned in towards town. Maybe if I got off with a bunch of other passengers, I could hide among them.

In this frantic mood, the ride went by slowly. I let my own stop go by and another and another until finally the bus was coming up to the end of the line.

But, like El Dorado, the end of the line was full of promise. It was the glittering spread of Harborplace, full of shops and offices, and, most importantly, people. Holding my breath as if I was plunging into a pool, I rushed off the bus into what I hoped would be a bustling crowd.

It was nearly four o'clock, too early for businesses to be letting out. Nonetheless, there were enough people around to give me a feeling of security. I headed for the stores that lined two sides of the harbor. I'd lose myself in them. It would take awhile to park the black car anyway, I reasoned smugly, then caught sight of it pulling into a suddenly opening spot along Light Street. Just my luck to be pursued by thugs blessed by the Parallel Parking gods. There wasn't time for regret. I ran toward the stores, and opened the door to what I hoped was my sanctuary.

Some tourists and early shoppers roamed the mall-like structure. I pretended to window shop while glancing over my shoulder. I would recognize the Lemming Lady with her bright red hair and out-of-control make-up. But what about her companion? I didn't know what he looked like. I could inadvertently stumble into his arms and not even know it.

Suddenly, every stranger looked threatening. A man with a line-backer build, goatee, and close-cropped hair stood admiring some sports paraphernalia. Was he the one? Another guy, spindly, unhealthy looking, and in need of a cigarette, eyed me from across the hall. Was he the male sidekick?

This was maddening. I raced through the mall, not wanting to linger near any man too long for fear he was the one. As I ran, my mind was racing, too, trying to determine what to do. Call Connie at her cell number! That was it. Just last night, she had said to use it in an emergency.

I spotted a store clerk on a cordless and meandered into her shop, a lingerie establishment filled with Wonderbras and square inches of silk that passed for panties. As soon as she saw me, and figured me to be a potential customer, she hung up. I pasted a bright, polite smile on my face and went up to the counter.

"I'm sorry to ask but I don't have any change. Could I use your phone to call my sister here in town to pick me up? I won't be more than a second."

She looked at me with an irritated grimace. Not only was I not going to buy anything. I wanted to use her phone for free. But she gave in and handed it to me reluctantly. I quickly punched in Connie's numbers, praying she had remembered to charge up and turn on the cell. Eureka! After two rings, her tentative voice came on the line.

"Hello?"

"Con, this is Bianca. I'm at Harborplace. Can you pick me up? I'll be at the corner of Pratt in ten minutes."

"What are you doing there? And why are you calling me on my cell phone?"

"I can't talk now. A nice lady is letting me use her phone," I said, smiling at the sales clerk. "Just pick me up in ten minutes. Please?" I didn't have to fudge the pleading tone in my voice. Heck, it bordered on desperate.

"Okay. I'll be there."

I hung up and thanked the sales clerk. All I had to do now was stay alive for the ten minutes it would take Connie to get here. Feeling better for having arranged the ride, I sauntered out into the mall with renewed confidence.

Until I ran right into a six-foot-three block of man whose imposing stature alone would scare even the bravest soul.

Chapter Six

The man loomed over me like an obelisk. He had thick dark hair and a squarish face that was rugged and tan. He wore a trench coat, a white shirt, and gray slacks. A slight bulge near his shoulder indicated he was packing some heat, as they say in detective novels about folks who carry guns.

He looked down at me with twinkling blue eyes, and smiled.

"Bianca, how's your mom?" Suddenly, it hit me. He was Steve Paluchek, a detective with the Baltimore City Police who had served with my dad and occasionally checked in on us. I liked him. He was like an uncle to me. And right now, he was the one person in the world I was happiest to see, because out of the corner of my eye I could now see Lemming Lady approaching.

"Fine, fine," I said, keeping track of the Lady. She had slowed down when she saw me talking with a stranger. I couldn't help noticing that her wardrobe selections had not improved. She still wore impractical boots and skin-tight pants, but today her choice had run to electric blue leggings topped by a black sparkly tube top under the leather jacket.

"Wish you would come over some time," I said, trying to keep the conversation going. To my relief, Detective Paluchek didn't seem to be in any hurry.

"I was thinking of stopping by soon. I was out of town at a diversity-training seminar for awhile. Then I had a broken arm that laid me up."

While Detective Paluchek went over the litany of reasons he hadn't visited, I finally saw the Invisible Man. He came up to Lemming Lady from the other side of the mall, joining her in trying to look nonchalant, pretending to scrutinize a display of handcrafted silver jewelry.

He was as frightening as I could have imagined, but not because of his physical stature. He was only a few inches taller than the woman and, though reasonably muscular, not overpowering. He had brown hair pulled into a tiny ponytail at the nape of his neck and he wore a long dark raincoat that nearly touched the top of his expensive-looking shoes. Everything about him looked expensive, from his coat and shoes to the glistening diamond stud in one ear, and the silk shirt I glimpsed when he moved.

But it was his face that really bothered me. Along one cheek was a two-inch scar starting right below his left eye and nearly meeting his nostril. His thin lips didn't smile and his squinty eyes looked like steel.

He was no longer Invisible Man. He was Ice Man, cold and cruel-looking, an image reinforced by the way he grabbed Lemming Lady's arm and steered her where he wanted to go without a second thought for her comfort or safety.

At some point, he made the decision to come my way, pulling her with him while she struggled to gain her balance. I had to think fast or he was likely to swoop by and snatch me without a second thought to the fellow I was talking with.

"Show me your badge!" I said quickly to the detective.

"What?" Paluchek looked confused.

"Your badge. I want to see if it's changed. I read somewhere that they were doing something different with the seal." Not bad for reasoning powers under panic conditions.

Detective Paluchek shrugged and pulled out the leather-covered wallet that held his badge. Meanwhile, I moved slightly so that when he displayed it, it would be in clear view of Lemming Lady and Ice Man. For added effect, I pulled a tissue from my pocket and dabbed at my eye to give the impression that I was a crying child tattling on my would-be stalkers.

It did the trick. As soon as Paluchek's badge glistened in the light, both my pursuers stopped dead in their tracks.

"Something the matter?" Detective Paluchek asked.

"No, just something in my eye," I nearly whispered to him. With my other hand, I fingered the badge. Despite my desperate circumstances, looking at the police badge conjured up melancholy feelings as I thought about how much I missed my dad. Even though I hadn't known him, I still had plenty of opportunities to miss him, like the many Father-Daughter dances at school where nice guys like Paluchek had to stand in.

"Looks the same. Must have been a false story," I said softly. My followers were slinking into the background. But I didn't want to leave the mall without protection. Connie should be arriving soon.

"You know, Connie would love to see you. She set up shop as a PI," I told him. "She's coming to pick me up. Should be here any minute. Why don't you walk me out and you can say hi. She'd really, really, *really* like that. She had some questions she wanted to ask you."

He looked confused but took the bait. "Okay. I'm not in any hurry. Where to?"

I took him by the arm and walked to the street with him, my own personal bodyguard who didn't even know he had the job. Lemming Lady and Ice Man dropped out of sight.

Paluchek and I ended up spending a bizarre twenty minutes on the curb waiting for my tardy sister. I must have told him every detail of my high school life, including stuff about Doug that I previously had divulged only to Kerrie. Funny what desperation does to a girl.

Whether or not the detective was confused by my sudden effusiveness wasn't clear to me. I was too focused on two things: keeping up a constant stream of banter so he would stay by my side, and scanning the crowd for my potential abductors. By the time Connie arrived, we had both forgotten about the "questions" she had to ask him, so I was able to make a clean escape with just a few pleasantries exchanged between my sister and Paluchek.

I wasn't so lucky with Connie alone. She peppered me with questions, but I stuck to a simple, inelegant story—I had fallen asleep on the bus and missed my stop. She couldn't quite understand why I didn't catch another bus, but I suspect she just chalked it up to my self-centered laziness. Okay by me. Better to reinforce her poor opinion of me than to swim with the fishes because of Ice Man and Lemming Lady.

At home, I quickly got dinner started per my mother's instructions, slapping together some ground beef and onion to make meat loaf and throwing it in the oven with a few potatoes to bake. It was almost therapeutic, taking out my fear and anger on the glob of ground beef in the bowl.

Then I called Kerrie. Thank goodness she was home. I finally spilled my guts about my adventures, even delighting in her screaming reactions to each new revelation. In fact, the more she screamed, the less fearful I felt. At the end of my tale, her voice became low, as if afraid of being overheard.

"Why didn't you tell the policeman you were being followed?" she asked.

"I guess I think that Sadie could be in trouble, and before I go blowing the whistle, I want to find out what the trouble is."

"We have to find out what's happening with her," Kerrie said.

"I know," I said. "But how?"

"Nobody knows where she lives or what her phone number is. And who knows if she'll come to school tomorrow."

"She could be in *big* trouble," I said.

"She could need our help."

"What if she doesn't come to school tomorrow, or the next day?"

"Rehearsals for *The Mikado* start next week," Kerrie said. "She has to show up then."

Round and round we went, mostly coming up with questions that had no answers. But by the time our marathon chat was over and the meat loaf was setting off the smoke alarm—a certain signal that it was done—we knew what we had to do. We had to find out where Sadie lived, or her phone number. And we had to find out why seedy folks like Lemming Lady and Ice Man were after her.

Easier said than done, it turned out. Sadie was not in school the next day or the day after. Kerrie and I continued our fruitless speculation over lunch and through long phone conversations and IM sessions on the computer. All to no avail. In fact, all this phone work did was make my sister mad at me, my mother worry about my school work, and Doug miss hooking up with me.

That's right. Doug *called me!* Surely you must hear my heart pounding because it's drowning out everything else on my end. He called on Wednesday night, the last respectable night for asking somebody out for the weekend.

In fact, Wednesday night is probably the night when phones across America are tolling with potential date-makers hanging onto every ring. Calling on Monday or Tuesday could appear too eager, too obsessive-compulsive.

Thursday, however, is too late. It communicates either a careless disregard for the potential date's schedule or feelings, or worse—it sends the message that the potential date is a second choice and the first choices already responded negatively on Wednesday.

Wednesday, you see, is the perfect date-making night. Not too eager. Not too late. Especially if you call early in the evening, which is what Doug, Love of My Life, did.

He called Wednesday at exactly 6:33 p.m., Eastern Standard Time. I know because I listened to the voice mail message about ten times before forcing myself to erase it. Saving it would provide too much ammunition for Tony.

After a brief pause, Doug had said, "Uh . . . this is Doug and if Bianca is in, could she call me back at . . .?"

Only problem was I didn't get the message until 10:53 p.m. Yes, I'm ashamed to admit it. I tied up our darn phone all night—but for a good cause, school work. Right after dinner, I got on the Internet, researching a paper.

Okay, okay, I was instant messaging Kerrie and Nicole at the same time.

Instant messaging can slow a body down when surfing the cyberwaves, so it was nearly 10:30 by the time I got off. And then I didn't think to check the voice mail until pulling the blankets over me. It made for a sleepless night thinking of Doug wondering why I hadn't called him back.

Double surprise. The first two people I ran into on Thursday morning were Doug and Sadie. They were talking, quietly and confidentially, in the room with all the lockers on the same floor as the cafeteria. I couldn't tell if I was pleased or angry to see them. I wanted to see them both. Just separately. Not together.

"Doug!" I said, trying to sound casually cheerful and instead coming off like a carnival barker reeling in a bumpkin. I ratcheted down the volume as I sauntered over to him and Sadie. "I was on the computer all night. Sorry I missed your call." Then I turned to Sadie. "Sadie, I need to talk to you."

"Yeah. Me, too," she said eagerly. But then she had the good sense to leave, telling me she'd see me around. I focused my attention on tall, handsome Doug, trying to quell my curiosity about Sadie's mysteries.

"I didn't check the messages until too late last night," I said, finally getting my voice down to a normal speaking tone.

"Well, I was wondering . . ." he began, and time seemed to divide into nanoseconds between that introduction and his next phrase, "what you were doing Saturday night. If you'd like to see a movie or something."

My mouth went dry and my hands got clammy. Here was paradise within my reach. All I had to do was grasp it. Doug was looking at me with an intense gaze, a gaze that said he was afraid I'd disappoint him. This was sweet, and I tried to memorize the moment to tell Kerrie about it later and to store it up for rainy days when happy memories are as good as chocolate. Well, almost as good.

"I'd love to do something, uh, go to a movie, yeah,

or something," I managed to sputter out with fantastic élan before the bell rang. And then we had to go our separate ways, neither of us with a game plan for this wondrous date, but both of us with the cozy sensation of having achieved a major mutual goal.

Chapter Seven

Here's the deal—when your boyfriend can't drive, you're left with two options, right? One of his older relatives can drive you. Or, you meet the guy at the appointed place, getting a ride with a relative of your own.

To Doug's credit, he offered me both choices. After much bashful stumbling over what we should do, when, and where, we finally settled on an action flick that began at seven at the Towson Cineplex. In a Friday night conversation before he ran off to work, he calmly laid out the possibilities.

"My dad can take us, if you want," he said, "or we can meet there. What's your pleasure?" Wow. That was smooth. I was impressed.

As much as I liked the idea of being picked up by a Doug surrogate, I wasn't a great small talker with older folks. With all the stress I had been under, dealing with Doug's dad just seemed like a bridge too far. I opted for Door Number Two and told him I'd meet him in front of the theater. He seemed relieved and suggested we meet at six at the mall so we could get a soda or something beforehand. We could then walk together down the road to the theater. This was nice—he was thinking of food, a romantic stroll, *and* a movie. What more could a girl want?

But let me back up to my stressed-out week. Sadie remained as elusive as ever. The first *Mikado* rehearsal was slated for Thursday after school, and I had hoped to hunker down with her in some auditorium seats while Mrs. Williston disorganized the practice.

Williston was really good at disorganizing. But this semester, she was disappointing me. She had a college student helping her and this girl had done a whiz-bang job of making sure not a moment was wasted. From the second we all marched into that auditorium until the minute we left it, we were corralled into place and had music seared into our brains. No time for small talk. Heck, this was too much like work.

I was surprised, though, to see that Sadie was not one of the leading ladies or even one of the understudies. She was stuck in the chorus with the rest of us Great Unwashed. While warbling through choruses about pretty maidens, the analytical side of my brain kicked in.

I had seen Sadie in tears twice in the past week. And both times, the weepiness seemed to come right after she was praised or rewarded for good work. First, there was the office visit where she had been given the note on her advanced placement standing in computer science and math.

Then, there was the audition in which it looked like Williston was offering her the Keys to the Theater Department Kingdom. But both times, Sadie had acted as if she were on the verge of being expelled, instead of being praised for good work. Curiouser and curiouser, I thought to myself.

After rehearsal, I missed my chance to talk with Sadie when she sped off immediately, practically running in the direction of the back of the school just as she had when Lemming Lady had been in pursuit.

Speaking of whom, neither of those ghastly folks were anywhere to be seen, and I began to think that my little ploy with Detective Paluchek had scared them off for good.

Kerrie road the bus home with me on Friday, so we had ample time to discuss the whole mess in between intense planning of my wardrobe for my big date with Doug.

"What do those two things have in common?" I asked Kerrie after passing along my observations of Sadie's two crying incidents.

"I don't know. Well, maybe parents. You have to get your parents' permission to take a lead role."

"I didn't know that," I said.

"Yeah, I guess Williston started a permission slip system last year after some kid agreed to sing the lead role in *Fiddler* and then had to bow out after three weeks of rehearsal because her family was taking a trip to France," explained Kerrie. "Now, Williston insists on parents signing off on leads."

"Why would that be such a big deal for Sadie?" I asked.

"Well, what about that woman who said she was Sadie's mom? Maybe Sadie is embarrassed by her," Kerrie commented.

I twisted my mouth up, and looked out the window

as we headed toward our neighborhoods. "I guess she could be Sadie's mom. I mean, it was hard to tell exactly how old she was."

I started to conjure up an image of home life in the Sinclair household. It wasn't a pretty picture. Lemming Lady screaming at Sadie to do this or do that, and the Ice Man standing in the background in his long cowboy coat just watching it all. I wondered if he was Sadie's mother's boyfriend. If that was true, no wonder the girl was strange.

"But getting her mother to sign a permission slip—since when is that such a big deal?" I asked. "I mean, I've forged my mother's signature once or twice when I forgot to get her to sign something I knew she'd sign anyway. You can't tell me Sadie wouldn't do the same."

Kerrie lapsed into thought. Just before her bus stop, she turned to me. "Maybe it isn't the permission slip," she said as she stood to get off. "Maybe she doesn't want her mother coming to school for anything."

After Kerrie got off, I thought about what she had said. It made a lot of sense. The note from the principal was requesting a meeting with Sadie's mother. That threw her into a tailspin. Then, she's on the verge of getting a leading role in the school play and she turns it down. Why? Not because her mother would have to sign off on it but because her mother would be expected to attend it. Sadie obviously didn't want her mother anywhere near the school.

If Lemming Lady really was her mother, who could blame her?

* * *

I now looked ahead to the best twenty-four hours of my short life. The mystery of Sadie had been solved, as far as I could tell. I had even figured out a reason why the Deadly Duo had chased me to Harborplace earlier that week. Sadie had probably run away from home for a night or two and they were looking for anyone who could lead them to her. When she returned, they gave up the chase. These unknowns now neatly tied up and compartmentalized, I resolved to become Sadie's friend and help her deal with what was obviously a dreadful home life.

I spent Saturday afternoon at Kerrie's house, giggling and chattering about what to wear to her Halloween costume party and whether or not Doug was going to try to kiss me sometime during our date. I had already solved my clothes problem for the big evening. Kerrie had helped me settle on my peasant blouse with black jeans. The only problem was that the weather was a little nippy, and none of my jackets looked good over the peasant blouse. I resolved just to be chilly. Sometimes you just have to suffer for the sake of beauty.

Everything was going well. I spent the rest of the afternoon with my family, and that managed to be pretty peaceful. Then—glory, hallelujah—I discovered that Connie would take me to my rendezvous, not Tony. Connie was much more sensitive to my desire to be places on time, whereas Tony—well, Tony just moved to the tune of a different band.

After dinner, the Hair Gods smiled on me and I was able to brush my honey brown locks into a devil-may-care style that was as close as I would ever come to model hair. I applied some light makeup with a subtle touch of glitter shadow on my eyes, and some rose-blush gloss on my lips. I had just about secured my hoop earrings when I heard the phone ring. A few seconds later, my mother called upstairs to me.

"Bianca! Phone!"

My heart dropped into my stomach. Everything had been going too well. It was probably Doug canceling. I could already feel the tears start to well behind my eyes. Stop it, I told myself. After all, if he's calling to cancel, it must be because something horrible has happened.

Somehow, that made me feel better.

"Hello?" I said tentatively in my best "don't-disappoint-me-now-you-heartless-toad" voice.

"Bianca? This is Sadie." Her voice was low, almost a whisper, and scared.

"Sadie! I heard you called the other day, but I didn't have your number!"

"Yeah, well, I forgot to leave it. I just wanted to thank you for the other day," she said awkwardly.

In the background, I thought I heard someone knocking on a door. It was hard to tell because she had the radio on, tuned to the same station I had playing in the background. I turned mine off.

"Is someone at your door?" I asked.

She paused, and it sounded as if she was walking to the door to see who it was. "No . . . no . . . probably somebody hammering something next door," she said so unsurely that I knew it was a lie.

"Sadie, who were those people looking for you the other day?"

Silence.

"Sadie? Are you there?"

"Yes. It's just that they . . ." The knocking started again.

"Look, Sadie, if that was your mother, you don't need to hide it."

I heard her sigh. Then: "Yes." The knocking stopped and I heard a buzzing, like an electronic doorbell, followed by more knocking, now quite insistent and loud. That was no next door neighbor doing home improvement. Someone wanted in and Sadie wasn't letting them.

"Sadie, what's going on? Do you need to get the door?" I asked.

"No, no." But her voice sounded frightened. "I have to go. This isn't a good time." I heard muffled shouting in the background, then the sound of a door opening and closing!

"Wait! Tell me where you live at least!" I shouted into the phone.

"Barrington . . ." she whispered frantically. Then I heard a woman's voice—it was the voice of Lemming Lady, I was sure of it. She was angry. "You should have let us in, you . . ." Then the phone went dead.

My palms were sweating as I thought of what to do. It was just before five.

"Connie!" I shouted in the hallway. My sister appeared from her room, romance novel in hand.

"What?"

"Can we leave now? I have an errand to run."

Connie looked at her watch and shrugged. "Sure. I wanted to pick some stuff up at the mall anyway." She went back into her room and reappeared a few seconds later with a shawl-collar sweater over her t-shirt and jeans. "You should wear a jacket," she said, digging through her purse for her car keys. "It's getting chilly."

"I'll be fine," I said and followed her out to the car. I really wanted to call Kerrie but there wasn't time. Plus, Connie might be able to help me. She was, after all, a PI. After we were on our way, I spilled the beans.

"Do you know a street called Barrington?" I asked.

"Why? I could look it up on a map for you," she said heading towards Towson. "What's on Barrington?"

I had no choice. I had to tell her. But I kept the information flow to a minimum. I didn't want to get Sadie in trouble and I didn't know yet what the full situation was. I only told Connie about Sadie's mom, the phone conversation, and my sense that something wasn't right.

"Is that why you wanted to leave early?" Connie asked me. "To find this Sadie person?"

"She sounded like she needed help, Con," I pleaded. "It would only take a minute, right? To drive past her house?"

"You don't even have a house number, for God's sake," Connie said, shaking her head. "All you have is 'Barrington.' You don't even know how many Barrington streets, avenues, roads there might be."

"Give me your cell phone," I said.

"What? It's in my purse."

I rummaged in her bag until I found it and punched in Kerrie's number. After explaining to her what I was doing and why, I asked her to look up Barrington Street on a map.

"Wait a minute," Kerrie said excitedly. "My dad has one of those criss-cross directories. You know the ones that list people by their addresses, not their names. Let me get it." It was typical of Kerrie to go for the more complicated solution. Instead of grabbing a map, or going online, she had to dig up a fancy directory.

But in a few seconds she was back on the phone and I could hear her whipping through the pages of a directory while she looked. "Barrington Street. Barrington Arms! That has to be it, Bianca! The Barrington Arms. It's a condo building in Towson, not far from the mall. That's probably it, but I don't see any Sinclairs listed."

"Maybe her mother's last name is different," I volunteered. "But where's Barrington Street? Check that out, too."

"Oh, no, I don't think so. It's in Glen Burnie. They've got a great new mall down there. With a Gap and everything."

I knew exactly what she meant. There was no need to stray far from one's home mall if it offered what you needed. If Sadie had been in the Towson mall, it was because she lived nearby, and probably in the Barrington Arms. The Barrington Arms, however, was a plush high-rise condo. Lawyers, financial gurus, and doctors lived there as well as a few retirees who had invested well. And the pedigree of most of the folks in the building was blue-blood Baltimore. Sinclair or not, Sadie didn't strike me as the Barrington Arms type.

"What are you going to do?" Kerrie said. "And what about your date?"

"I have some time," I reassured her. "My sister and I will just do a quick drive-by to see if everything is okay."

"Bianca," Kerrie said, and I thought for sure she

was going to tell me to be careful, "what are you wearing—the peasant blouse or the silvery tee?"

"The peasant blouse," I told her. "Look, I gotta go. I'll call you."

"You better!"

We hung up and I gave the scoop to Connie, who just raised her eyebrows and stepped on the gas. "Okay, sis," she said, "we'll do a little look-see at the Barrington Arms if it'll make you feel better."

The Barrington Arms was a huge curved building on a prime piece of real estate in Towson. Its rows of windows looked like some crazed jack-o-lantern's teeth, with some of them blacked out and others shining brightly. As I stared at it, I wondered how I would ever know which lights belonged to Sadie's apartment.

"Come on," Connie said after parking the car. "Let's go inside."

We walked along the darkened street toward the large, brightly lit foyer. No doorman. Hmmm, I would have thought a ritzy place like this would have a doorman. But then I saw the rows and rows of buttons next to intercom speakers. Obviously, we wouldn't get in the front door without being buzzed in. And we wouldn't get buzzed in without knowing which apartment to buzz.

Nearing the door, I noticed a big expensive black car parked right out front. It was the Deadly Duo's car! Man, oh man, they sure had lots of great parking karma.

Connie looked at the names next to the buzzers.

"We're in luck," she said. "I know one of these."

She pressed the button next to "Glyndon, A." She pressed it again. And again. Nothing. A. Glyndon was out.

"Guess we're not in luck," I murmured sarcastically.

"Hold your horses," Connie shot back and made a twirling motion with her finger as she decided which button to land on. She ended up on "Houston, C." A few seconds later, an elderly woman's voice answered "Yes?"

"Hi, Alex? It's Connie!"

"Who?" the woman asked, obviously perplexed.

"Connie! Is this Alex Glyndon? I'm sorry. I must have pressed the wrong number. Alex is expecting me." She used her most innocent voice to ask the woman to let us in, and I fully expected the older woman, after being smothered in Connie's charm, to buzz the door open. But it was not to be. With a final harrumph, the woman said caustically, "Well, I guess you better wait until your friend gets in." Ouch.

Before I had a chance to chide Connie about this failure, a dashing older man raced through the lobby and pushed open the door. Before it could close, Connie grabbed me, flashing a triumphant smile as if she had planned it this way, and escorted me into the posh lobby.

Covered with a rose-patterned rug, The Barrington Arms lobby had potted palms and chairs placed casually throughout the space in conversation groups that I couldn't imagine ever being used.

"Who's Alex Glyndon?" I asked her as we waited for the elevator. "And where are we going?"

"Alex is a lawyer. I've done some work for him. And we're just going fishing, sweetheart. We're going to take a quick stroll through all the hallways of Barrington Arms."

The elevator arrived and she pressed the button for the top floor. When we reached our destination, she silently but briskly led the way through the hall.

"What are we looking for?" I asked, struggling to keep up. I had never seen my sister so purposeful before. I was impressed.

"Not looking. Listening. For an argument, for a familiar voice. Shut up and get to work," she said.

She strolled the halls, pausing a little in front of each door and looking at me inquisitively to see if I heard anything. Nothing on the top floor. And nothing on the floor below, or the one below that. Silent as a tomb, as a matter of fact. The Barrington Arms did not appear to be a jumpin' kind of place.

But on the next floor, I heard music, a song by Destiny's Child, just the kind of song often played by my favorite radio station, the station that had been playing in the background at Sadie's place during her phone call to me. A pop song meant someone young was behind that door. I stopped, holding up my hand to my sister to indicate this door had promise. I leaned my head against it, listening intently. A low murmur of troubled voices came from inside along with the sounds of muffled sobs. Was that Sadie crying? Connie pulled me aside.

"What is it?" she asked me in a whisper.

"The radio station. I think." I grabbed my sister's purse. "Do you have your phone on you?" I found it before she could answer and punched in Kerrie's number while Connie just stared at me both amused and annoyed.

"Kerrie," I whispered into the phone when my friend answered. "Turn on WKDY . . . don't ask . . . just turn it on . . . I'm in hurry. Now tell me what song is on." When Kerrie confirmed it was the Destiny's Child hit, I knew with every fiber of my being that we had located Sadie's home. I told my sister.

"You go hide around the corner," she instructed me. "Sadie and her mother would recognize you." I did as she told me and peered around to watch her knocking on the door. It opened slowly after someone called through asking her name, which she gave as "Constance Moran from St. John's."

"I'm so sorry to disturb you," she said in a perky, business-like voice. "I'm Constance Moran from the Alumni Association of St. John's Academy. I live in 803 and I'm trying to visit all new St. John's students in my neighborhood and I understand that Sadie Sinclair lives here." She even pulled a piece of paper out of her purse and appeared to be consulting it as she said Sadie's name. She also mispronounced it—a nice touch—saying "Sah-dee" instead of "Say-dee."

Someone said something to Connie that I couldn't make out. Then Connie, perky smile still on her face, backed away. "I'm sorry. I'll be sure to try again. Let me leave a card . . ."

She rummaged through her purse for a few seconds. "Well, I can't seem to put my hands on one right now, but I can leave one when I come back. I'm so glad you're at St. John's. It's a terrific school, isn't it?" It didn't take long for the door to shut on her.

Chapter Eight

"Well?" I asked Connie, coming out of my hiding place and joining her as we walked down the hall together.

"Well, if that's Sadie Sinclair in there, she's not harmed as far as I could see. Just a little teary-eyed. She was in the distance. A man was standing by the window looking out. And a redhead spoke to me. Had a cigarette voice and too much makeup."

"Yeah, that was her," I said.

"That was who, her mother?"

"I guess. So you don't think anything was out of the ordinary? That's a relief." My mind immediately turned to thoughts of my date. If we hurried, I'd get there right on the dot of six.

Just as we rounded the corner to the elevator bank, we heard a door open. Looking back, we saw it was Sadie's door. Connie grabbed me and pulled me forward. "Come on. If they see you with me, they'll know I was faking."

We ran silently on the plush carpet and Connie hit

the elevator button. We couldn't turn back. The staircase was behind us, in full view of Sadie's door. We could hear footsteps in the hall as we waited, an excruciatingly long three seconds until the doors whooshed open.

But it was too late. They also had heard the doors open and were racing to catch the same elevator. Just as they rounded the corner, Connie pulled my face into her shoulder and whispered emphatically, "Start sobbing."

I responded like a robot and pretended to cry while she whipped out her cell phone with her other hand and faked a conversation. "Uh-huh . . . yeah. We're on our way now . . . are you sure? Okay . . . okay . . ."

I could tell the others had boarded the elevator, but I couldn't see them because my face was buried in my sister's shoulder.

"Her dog just died," she said to them as the elevator started moving. "Was with her all her life." Geez, she even put a catch in her throat. "My sister is taking it pretty bad."

After an interminable ride, during which Connie comforted me in halting tones, we finally reached the lobby and walked out behind them. I lifted my head an inch and saw all three of them together. Sadie was walking ahead of the other two as if she knew where she was going. They didn't get in the car but headed down the street instead. Connie held me back and just stared at them.

"There is definitely something weird here," she said looking at them walking together.

"I think you ruined my hairdo," I said, touching my crushed strands.

"Come on!" She grabbed my hand and followed the three down the dark streets.

"Con, my date!" I hissed at her.

"Don't worry. I'll get you there. We're one minute away from the mall, for God's sake."

With that reassurance, I happily joined in the chase. Connie was staying close to buildings and ducking into store overhangs every few seconds. No one else was out and about so the chances of being caught by Sadie and her crew were high. We had to proceed cautiously and at a fair distance. At the corner of York and Dunston Lane, they stopped.

Connie pulled me back suddenly into a store door, but it had one of those old-fashioned gates pulled over it to keep thieves out. We were in the middle of the block and like sitting ducks. If we didn't do something soon, they could look back and see us. Connie tugged at the gate.

To our amazement, it gave way and we were able to slip behind it, into a small entrance way. We cowered in the shadows as Connie pulled out a small pair of binoculars from her purse, crouched, and looked through the store's glass showcase down the street.

"What are they doing?" I asked, pulling at her arm.

"They're at a bank. It looks like Sadie is using an ATM machine."

"She's giving them money?"

"Wait a minute! Don't jiggle my arm. This is hard enough." A few seconds later, she put the glasses down. "Sadie just gave them an envelope. My guess is it's filled with money. She's paying them off for some reason."

"Why would she pay off her mom?" I said.

"Maybe that woman isn't her mother," Connie whispered.

"Sadie told me she is." But then I remembered my conversation with Sadie and how noncommittal and distracted she had been. "At least I think she is."

"Shhh! They're turning back!"

"Let's get out of here," I yelped.

"Too late. We have to hide." Connie looked around our dark corner and grabbed a grungy welcome mat. It was black rubber with rough grippers on one side that held all sorts of unmentionable dirt and bugs. To my horror, Connie pulled this mat in front of herself and grabbed me underneath it.

"My blouse!" I hissed to no avail as Connie mashed her purse way back in the corner where it couldn't be seen. She kicked off her shoes and tore mine off, too, shoving everything back into the corner.

"Shut up," she hissed right back.

To any passer-by who happened to glance our way, we just looked like two homeless wretches sleeping off the night in a warm doorway. A few minutes later, we heard the three walk by. When their footsteps faded out of earshot, Connie pulled the gross mat off of us and laid it on the ground, kicking up a storm of dust that made me sneeze.

"Be quiet," she warned. "They might still hear you." She stood and reached for the gate to open it.

"I'm a mess," I whined, feeling awfully sorry for myself. Here I had planned a look that was so perfect, so casual, yet so alluring. So neat, yet so carefree. So attractive, yet so . . .

"That's the least of your worries," Connie said as she yanked at the gate.

And yanked. And yanked again.

It was locked. My eyes widened and my pulse raced as I realized our predicament.

"You got us in here!" I nearly shouted at her. "What's the problem?"

"The gate was accidentally left open," she said, fiddling with its lock. "I must have locked it when I pulled it shut on us."

"Connie! I have a date! My first date with Doug! I can't be trapped here. It's getting late! What time is it anyway?" I paced our small cage like an animal, unable to really believe that I was trapped with my sister in a dingy doorway while Doug waited for me at the mall. Connie, meanwhile, let out a curse as she unsuccessfully tugged on the gate after another attempt to maneuver the lock.

"Forget about your date! What do we tell the police when they find us here? Oh, gee, Officer, I thought it would be funny to see what it feels like to be in a zoo? That'll sit real well with the PI licensing folks." She worked at the gate lock with fervor, trying various keys and other pointy objects from her key ring that I didn't know she had.

"Guess you were absent on Lock Picking Day," I said sarcastically, folding my arms over each other. I didn't dare look at my blouse. I knew it was probably smudged with dirt from the rubber mat. And my hair—my hair felt like a matted rug that had a certain odor now, what I'd call *L'Air du Wet Dog*. I was sure to make a big impression on Doug. That is, after he forgave me for being late.

"You could help, you know," she muttered between clenched teeth. "Grab the gate and hold it up a little. If I can jimmy the latch . . ."

I did as she said. And I did it again and again. But a quarter of an hour later, we were still trapped and I was beginning to see my dating life flash before my eyes. It didn't take long.

"All right," she said emphatically. "That's it. Time to call in the Marines." She grabbed her purse and pulled out her cell phone, hit a speed dial number and pursed her lips while she waited for someone to pick up.

"Hi. I need your help . . ."

For a hour, Connie and I hid in the shadows to avoid the gaze of occasional drivers, and I whined about the fact that we were trapped in the doorway of a weird comic book store instead of the vintage clothing shop across the street ("clothes for the tragically hip"). Finally, a hunky specimen of the *genus manus* arrived.

Despite my frantic state, I couldn't help but admire this fellow's appearance and my sister's ability to summon such a guy with the briefest of calls. His name was Kurt and Connie seemed to know him really well.

Kurt was over six feet and built like a muscle man. He had a military close-shave haircut, a nose that looked like it had been mashed once in a fight, an anchor tattoo on his left upper arm, and thick lips.

But his eyes were so blue I could see their color even through the shadows, and he was kind, and smelled like English Leather after-shave, which was always a favorite of mine. He almost made me forget about Doug. Actually, not even near.

He was Connie's "friend," first of all, and too old for me. My guess is he was maybe thirty-five. He pulled some metal objects from his pocket, and soon had the gate open.

"That was a tough one," he said. "Took me two minutes."

Connie smiled at him and patted him on the arm. "So I shouldn't feel bad for not getting it?"

"It was rusted. Show me what you were using."

This, I decided, was no time for a comparison of lock-picking tools. I had a guy of my own waiting for me. At least I hoped he was still waiting for me. I could barely bring myself to look at my watch. When I did, I let out a muted scream. It was seven-thirty, an hour and a half after the time I had said I would meet Doug.

"Connie! My date!" I pleaded with her.

"Okay, okay," she said to me, brushing dust off my shoulder.

"I can give you a ride," Kurt said, pointing to his Jeep. Connie graciously sat in the back so I could hop out of the front seat the second we got to the mall. Kurt pulled away from the curb with the speed and precision of someone used to maneuvering vehicles through tricky situations. In less than a minute, we were not only at the mall, but at the exact entrance closest to the prearranged meeting spot. Maybe, just maybe, Doug was still there.

"Do you want me to wait?" Kurt asked as I unfolded myself from the front seat.

"No, no thanks."

Connie piped up from the back seat. "You can call me if you need a ride."

With that optimistic send-off, I ventured into the mall.

I was already too late. I couldn't risk stopping in a ladies room to undo the damage of my evening of investigating. So, my plan was to locate Doug, give him a breezy kiss on the cheek that would make him oblivious to the fact that I looked and smelled like I had crawled out of a sewer, and then excuse myself, making a quick trip to the ladies room, where I would spray myself with perfume, brush my hair, reconfigure my make-up, and assess the damage to my self-esteem.

Good thing I had to think of that plan. It kept me from thinking of the inevitable—that I wouldn't hook up with Doug at all. Why should he wait nearly two hours for a no-show, I thought mournfully as I scanned the area in front of the food court where we'd agreed to meet.

I walked around hoping against hope to find Doug window shopping while he waited for me. No luck. I ran to the door we would have taken to walk to the theater, and scanned the crowd there. Still no Doug. I wandered slowly back to the Food Court, a lump in my throat now as I contemplated my loss. What must he have thought?

But wait! Maybe he had gone into the movie. I ran back to the mall door, and jogged down the road to the theater. I should have had Kurt drop me off there!

Breathlessly, I shelled out the money for a ticket, giving myself a quick surreptitious spray of vanilla bean body mist, and went into the flick we had agreed to see. While flames and explosions lit up the screen, I methodically looked over each row. Couples, groups together, no individuals sitting alone, no head that looked like Doug's.

I turned around, skulking out of the theater and toward the pay phone in the lobby. First, I called Tony to see if anyone had called. But I got the voice mail, a sure sign he was tying up the line or mom was on the computer. If Doug had tried to call me, he would have gotten the same non-response. Then, I dialed Connie's cell phone. She picked up on the second ring and I could hear the sound of traffic.

"Hi," I said sadly. "It's me."

"He wasn't there," she said softly. She actually sounded sympathetic. "Don't worry. I'll come back. Where are you?"

A cheeseburger, chocolate milk shake, Boardwalk Fries, and chocolate mousse cake later, Connie and I were on our way home. She had treated me to a meal at the Food Court, even forgoing her health food diet to share the fries. And, she handed over her cell phone so I could try reaching Doug, but his line was busy both times I dialed.

It was nearly ten o'clock by the time we got home, my stomach full of the unsatisfying substitute for losing out on the big date. I didn't like to call people whose family habits I wasn't aware of after nine-thirty. so I fought off the temptation to try Doug again before crawling into bed.

Needless to say, I didn't sleep well that night. As I

tossed and turned, I thought of the different ways I could explain myself to him the next day, trying to make my story sound as pitiful as it really was.

The next morning, we all went to church together. We don't always manage to pull this off. Sometimes, Connie doesn't go. Or Tony says he's going to the later Mass (but I know he just hangs out for forty-five minutes at the Dunkin' Donuts; I've smelled chocolate éclair on his breath), so it's just Mom and me. I figure it's the least I can do for Mom, and besides, you never know, right?

We got home close to eleven and I immediately checked the phone. No messages. Connie started reading the newspapers and watching the Sunday talk shows. Tony grabbed some books from his room and headed out to the college library. Mom tried to interest me in going to the fabric store with her to buy material for a tablecloth, which was just a subterfuge for getting me interested in sewing a Christmas dress. Ordinarily, I would have jumped at the chance. Not today.

As soon as she left, I went up to my room, cordless phone in hand, and dialed Doug's number. My hands were clammy as I heard it ring. By the third ring, I was getting ready to leave a cheerful message apologizing and asking him to call me when he answered the phone with a listless "Hello?"

"Doug!" I nearly shrieked into the receiver. "It's Bianca. Look, I'm really, really sorry about last night. I am *so* sorry. You just can't imagine how sorry I am . . ."

"What happened?" he asked. "I waited for an hour and a half."

"Oh man, you must have just missed me. I mean I must have just missed you. It was car trouble. My sister Connie drove me. We were stuck for over an hour. I went to the mall afterwards and looked all over and tried to call you."

"Yeah, well." He didn't sound happy. Something was not going right here. I had apologized, given a perfectly credible explanation, and he sounded like I had sucker punched him right in the gut.

"I'll make it up to you," I improvised, coming up with a plan that was both practical and brilliant. "I'll treat *you*. What about next weekend? Let's try for that same movie again . . ."

He didn't say anything. Nothing. Silence . . . that was not golden. Anything but.

"Or this afternoon," I said, the cheer leaving my voice like air escaping a deflating balloon. "I'm free. I could get Connie to pick you up."

It was hopeless. He clearly wasn't interested. Obviously, I had committed a mortal sin against Doug's dating commandments.

"I'm really sorry, Doug," I said, sincerity taking over. I was practically in tears. "I didn't mean to be late."

"Yeah, well . . ." he said again. Someone shouted in the back ground. "Look, I gotta go. My mom wants to use the phone."

After he hung up, I kept the phone pressed to my ear as tears streamed down my face. It was so unfair. I got tied up. I was late. Accidents happen. What if I had been in a real accident? What if I had been lying in the middle of the street bleeding? What if I had been calling him from my hospital bed? Would he have acted like such a . . . a cold fish *then?* My vision blurred by crying, I grabbed for a tissue and punched in Kerrie's number. When she answered, I told her the whole gruesome tale.

Chapter Nine

Once again I came to school on a Monday waiting with bated breath (what the heck is "bated breath" anyway?) for news from the grapevine. Kerrie had managed to comfort me on Sunday by swearing to find out what was going on with Doug. She assured me that Doug was a nice guy, incapable of being the kind of jerk who would cut a girl off simply because she hadn't been able to make a date. Kerrie promised, with an intensity usually reserved for oaths before a law enforcement officer, that she would talk to Marsha, who would talk to Doug, and all would be crystal clear on Monday.

While that had consoled me for a short time—long enough to catch up on much-needed sleep during an afternoon nap—the reality of the situation had hit me like cold water Sunday evening.

What in the world would make Doug turn on me? If he acted that way simply because I stood him up, and for good reason, too (I kept reminding myself), was he really the kind of guy I wanted to hitch my heart to? That started me in on a whole downward spiral of thoughts. After all, you want to think your first crush is your One True Love, right? And it's bad enough to deal with the fact that maybe he isn't, but usually this occurs after months and months of dating, not before you actually go out on your first evening together.

I was just gifted and talented at dating, I guess, jumping over all those interim steps and zipping to the heart-breaking finale without even a hug or a kiss from the guy in question.

Somehow, this newfound precociousness didn't make me feel any better. I was downright miserable by bedtime Sunday night.

But Monday was a new day, filled with expectations, opportunities, hope—the first day of the rest of my . . . whatever.

Kerrie came breezing into the locker hall exactly fifty-nine seconds before the first bell was to ring, which almost made me scream at her in indignation, but I was too eager to hear the scoop, and she had to have it. She *had* to.

She had a smile on her face. Good sign. Her eyes were wide. Another good sign.

"Well?" I asked with no explanation. She knew what I wanted. She quickly threw the dial of her locker in a spin and began talking.

"Well, Doug is mad at you." She put her lunch inside and began rearranging books.

What a revelation, I wanted to shout. Doug is mad at me. I never would have guessed. Silly me. I had been holding out hope that it really was his evil twin on the phone with me on Sunday.

"Yeah, but why? I mean, I apologized."

"He saw you," Kerrie said, smiling. "You sly fox."

Uh-oh. Kerrie was beginning to scare me. What in the world did she mean? The bell buzzed and I thought I would have to kidnap her right then and there to get the full story. I wasn't going another second without knowing.

"What do you mean? Come on, I'm confused, and I've got to get to class."

She slammed her locker shut and gave the lock a twirl. "He saw you with that hunk you're obviously keeping secret from me," she said sassily.

That hunk? Kurt. Now it all became clear. Doug had told me he left the mall just around the time I was arriving. He must have seen me get out of the front seat of Kurt's Jeep with Connie hidden in the back. He thought I was two-timing him before we even had a chance to one-time it together.

Part of me was—I have to admit it—pleased. Doug was jealous. And if he was jealous, that meant he—cared. But part of me was annoyed. Why hadn't he just told me what he'd seen?

"Why didn't he just say something to me?" I asked as we hurried to our home rooms.

"You know how guys are—from Mars," Kerrie said and flew into her homeroom.

Doug might be from Mars, but I felt stuck in orbit between the twin moons "Confused" and "Frustrated." I couldn't figure out a way to tell him the truth without it sounding artificial. *Oh, Doug, I forgot to mention,* I heard myself saying in a sing-song voice, *I got a ride to the mall with my sister's tattooed friend Kurt.*

Who would use that as a conversation ice-breaker? Yet this was my day to set the situation right. We shared a lunch hour. If I waited until Wednesday, it would be too late. Instinctively, I knew that a three-day lapse would cause his original assessment of the night to set, as in concrete, unmovable except by a huge explosion.

All this fretting about Doug almost made me forget to fret about Sadie. I saw her midmorning in Honors French. She looked tired but none the worse for wear. In fact, in some ways, she looked better. Her hair was darker—she must have put a rinse on it—so her roots didn't show through so badly. And her skin was brightened by a little blush. She looked like she was trying to be normal, a good sign. At lunch, she sought me out as we entered the cafeteria together. Catching up with me, she tapped my arm.

"Thanks again," she said shyly.

"Is everything okay? My sister and I—we were worried about you."

"I know," Sadie smiled. "Connie Moran, right?"

Sadie knew! She knew it was us at her apartment the other night.

"Pretty silly of us, huh?" I said.

"No, I appreciated it. In fact, I was touched," she said, beaming at me. She had a nice smile that made her face look innocent and sweet. "Everything's okay."

I couldn't tell if she was lying, and I was about to ask her about the ATM adventure, when she caught sight of Doug, a/k/a "Martian Man." He waved at her. I dropped to my knees sobbing.

Not really. But I did get that sinking feeling—the

same one I had when I heard she had been at his house. Oh heck, I was tired of being coy. Direct questions were the ticket, I decided.

"You and Doug have something going on?" I asked as casually as I could muster, hoping my tremulous voice didn't give me away.

"What? No. I thought you and Doug were an item," she said.

"Well, I don't know. I heard you were at his house."

"Yeah. To do math homework. He needed some help. Mrs. Baumgarten paired us up. One of those team learning deals."

Relief flooded over me like rain after a drought. I had to do everything in my power to keep from breaking into the "Hallelujah Chorus" right then and there. I was ready to dance on tables, to scream it to the mountain tops—Doug, the Martian Man, is still *mine!*

"So," I continued, "do you go often?" I cleared my throat.

"No. We're done. Why? Do you want me to put in a good word for you?"

A good word for me? From Sadie, who had helped Doug with his math homework? Now, that held promise.

"Actually, you could . . ." I explained how Connie and I had had "car trouble" and Kurt had come to our rescue, and how Doug had seen me with Kurt and misunderstood.

"No problem," Sadie said assuredly. "I can spin that story any way you want." She sauntered over to Doug's table, more confident than I had ever seen her, a new Sadie, a Sadie very comfortable telling stories.

My life was back on track. I spent the afternoon and the next few days successfully pretending to be normal. Sure, Doug and I hadn't completely patched things up, but he didn't look away from me when I passed him in the hallways, and once I could have sworn he even smiled at me when he caught sight of me in the chorus rehearsal.

Or maybe it was a grimace. Or maybe he just had something in his eye.

Every night I was on tenterhooks waiting for him to call me and ask me out again. But by now I was used to this state of nervous anticipation and it didn't shake me, at least not too much.

Kerrie insisted, in phone calls, IMs, emails, and school chats, that Doug was a typical guy (from Mars) and would have trouble backing down and admitting he was wrong. I should give him time, she insisted, and if that didn't work, I should just try asking him out, repeating my offer to make up the lost date.

It sounded like a good plan—Kerrie was always good for plans—so I stuck to it, even though it nearly drove me crazy and took every ounce of my self-control.

Luckily, or maybe unluckily, my family suddenly got a bad case of Donna Reed disease. That's where we all start acting like characters in some old 1950s sitcom, filled with brotherly and sisterly love and activities that have all of us buzzing around our hive like bees on a deadline.

My mother coerced me into going to the fabric store with her again and I actually let her buy five yards of hunter green velvet for a holiday dress for me. Connie told me privately that she was looking into who owned Sadie's condo. She also talked about hiring me in her office during the summer. Suddenly, I had visions of working side-by-side with her on important life-and-death cases.

And Tony—well, come to think of it, Tony was kind of immune from this strange affliction, so he stuck to his usual schedule of pretending he didn't know us even when he was in the same house.

So the week passed like a kind of timeless limbo. I was out of the house enough to keep my compulsion to call Doug under wraps. But I have to admit, I felt blue every time I came home and checked the messages, only to find no "Doug-a-gram" waiting to cheer me.

Kerrie insisted that he wouldn't be the type to leave a message if he was going to apologize, but I wasn't so sure. A couple times, I did the old *69 routine to find out if he had called, but I never caught his number showing up. Just a few "sorry, that number is not available or private" messages squawked at me, and I assumed they belonged to Sadie. Why the heck wouldn't she just leave her number?

The weekend came around with no call from Doug. I was desperate, depressed, and nearly delusional. I imagined all sorts of scenarios—from Sadie lying to me about her relationship with Doug to . . . well, trust me, you don't really want to know.

We had a play practice at school that weekend, the first of many. I was beginning to regret letting Hilary con us all into auditioning. Gilbert and Sullivan wasn't my cup of tea in the first place, and now it meant going to school on Saturdays.

Plus, I was beginning to think in those darn patter-song couplets. *If Dougie doesn't call me soon/I'll descend into an endless gloom/So please be kind, oh Mister Doug/And give this girl more than a shrug.*

Okay, okay. So I'm not good at the patter thing. But you get the idea. The only silver lining about the rehearsal was that Doug would be there.

Or so I thought. When Kerrie and I walked into the auditorium on Saturday afternoon, he was nowhere to be seen. And he didn't show up for the whole boring three-hour stretch of rhyming lines and tongue twisting choruses. I was in a pretty bleak mood after the rehearsal, so Kerrie decided to cheer me up.

Of course, it involved a plan.

"My dad will pick me up when I call him," she said as we left the school building. "Why don't we go out to Charles Village? There's a really neat vintage clothing store there. We could probably find all sorts of things for costumes." Kerrie was really into the costume thing. My guess is she had thought about visiting this store all week. In fact, she might have been planning this trip since last Easter.

"I don't have any money."

"I'll lend you some if you see something you like. I've got my mother's charge card."

Kerrie always had her mother's charge card. I think it was really Kerrie's card but she was embarrassed about flaunting her family income.

I agreed to go. After all, Doug hadn't called me yet and he hadn't shown up at rehearsal. That all conformed with Delusional Scenario #54, the one where he's called in to work extra hours because some co-worker has run off to Tahiti with the boss's daughter.

Who could leave their employer in such a pinch, right? Doug was a great guy.

Kerrie had mapped out this plan carefully enough to know that the bus we needed to catch was a street over, behind the school. We started walking that way, talking aimlessly about homework, clothes, the weather, the rehearsal—anything except Doug. As we got closer to the bus stop, Kerrie stopped and pulled back behind a scrawny city tree.

"Hey, look," she said staring down the block. I followed her gaze. There was Sadie, oblivious to our presence, getting into a car. Getting into the *driver's* side of a car. Starting the engine, pulling out into the street.

I yanked at Kerrie, pulling her down behind some parked cars so Sadie wouldn't see us as she drove off. As the vehicle sped away, I got up and squinted at the back, memorizing the license plate number. It wasn't a Maryland tag. It was a California plate.

"That is weird," Kerrie said in awestruck tones under her breath. "She's driving already."

For a few moments, we didn't say anything to each other. Too many thoughts were cascading through our brains simultaneously. Was Sadie older than we thought? Or was the driving age lower in California? But then Kerrie articulated the one thought that both of us were zeroing in on.

"Sadie is not who we think she is."

Chapter Ten

The trip to the vintage clothing store evaporated like mist on a fall morning. We stood on the sidewalk gawking, or maybe it was more like meditating—the goal of which was to pull from the cosmos the telltale clues to who the real Sadie Sinclair was. We didn't like feeling duped. We had helped her, reached out to her. And she wasn't telling us something. She was leaving out some vital piece of information. We had to find out what it was.

Well, at least I did. Things had gone so wrong in my life, specifically the Doug date debacle, that I felt a strong urge to find a scapegoat. Sadie would do.

"Come on," I yelled at Kerrie, grabbing her arm and marching back toward the school building.

"Bianca, what are you doing?"

"We're going sleuthing," I said, taking long strides. I wanted to get there before Williston closed up.

"What? How? What are we looking for and how are we going to find it?" Kerrie sounded hysterical.

Happy, but hysterical. Knowing how much she liked plans, I made one up myself.

"First we're going to get into the school office. Then we're going to look up the file on a Miss Sadie Sinclair, recently of California, and alleged high school sophomore."

That did the trick and Kerrie followed enthusiastically. When we got back to the school, the doors to the auditorium wing were still open. In the lobby, we could hear Williston and the accompanist rehearsing with Hilary and the other leads. As the piano clanked out its tinny background music, I pulled Kerrie with me, trying to imitate my sister Connie's confident style the night we . . . actually, I didn't want to think about that night much.

We went upstairs and down the long, dark first-floor hall. The office was near the central stairwell, the last door on our right. Like all the doors, it had a pebbled glass window on its upper section. No lights shone through, indicating it was empty. And locked. I twisted the knob to and fro just to confirm the obvious.

"Bianca, I don't know . . ."

"Shhhh!" I knelt down and peered into the room through the keyhole. But there was nothing to see except the beige wallboard of the countertop that greeted the unfortunate students called to the office from time to time.

"We can't break in," Kerrie whined at me. What a disappointment she was turning out to be in the PI department.

But she did have a point. I couldn't break in. I didn't know how. I stood up. "When brawn doesn't work, use brains," that was my motto—one that I just made up.

"Okay, okay," I said to Kerrie. "Here's the plan. You go back to Williston. Tell her you forgot—you were supposed to pick up . . ." I bent down again and scanned the counter top in the room beyond. It was loaded with forms. "Your PSAT application! Your father will kill you if you don't get it done this weekend. You just have to have it. Come on, Kerrie, you can do it!" I said it as if I were a football coach sending the team out to take on a bunch of all-stars.

But Kerrie bought it. Probably because I started out by telling her it was a plan. While I waited, she happily marched off toward the auditorium. I could have gone with her, of course, but I didn't want to interfere with her performance. Really.

After a brief interval, I heard the music stop in the auditorium. I held my breath, hoping that Kerrie was going to come back with the key without Miss Williston in tow. A couple minutes later, Kerrie appeared, key dangling in front of her, and a triumphant grin on her face. She ran the last few feet to the door and giggled when I unlocked it.

Once inside, I walked behind the counter to the long rows of filing cabinets that held the secrets of our young lives—the parent-teacher conference notes, the report cards, the detention notices. What power I had in my hands right now, I thought, as Kerrie, standing next to me, waited for my latest directive.

"What's next?" she whispered.

"What's next is you grab a form off the counter and take the key back to Williston," I said. "I don't want her sending someone up here to get it from you."

"But what about Sadie's file?"

"I'll stay inside here and look for it. Close the door behind you and turn off the light. When you come back, tap on the door three times like this." I knocked softly on the desk behind me, two quick beats followed by a pause and the final beat. "And I'll let you in."

"Okay." She dutifully picked up the form and ran off, closing and locking the door behind her. I was glad she wasn't with me. I didn't want her getting into trouble too if I was caught. Going through student files was serious business and I knew I could be expelled if someone came in and caught me. I started thinking of possible explanations to offer if that happened.

My mother asked me to bring a copy of my report card home? I couldn't remember what my last Stanford Achievement Scores were? I saw a shadow and thought I'd investigate? Extraterrestrials had landed? The voices in my head told me to do it?

They were all lame lines, so I kept thinking of other excuses as I approached the filing cabinets.

Let me elaborate on that—the *locked* filing cabinets. Good grief, I thought, the whole world is locked up tight like a prison. But wait a minute. The key would probably be nearby.

I turned to the desk and slid open the pencil drawer in the center. It was neatly organized with rubber bands and paper clips and pennies in different plastic compartments. And small keys, just the kind you use to open file cabinets. I pulled them out and started trying them on the drawers. It didn't take long to get the right one. It unlocked a whole row. I found the "S's" and started searching.

When I found Sadie's file, I wished I'd had a camera so that I could take photos of the pages, even though there weren't that many of them. Compared to most of the fat, paper-stuffed folders for the other students, Sadie's was pretty slim. All it contained was a letter from her mother, whose last name, I noted with surprise, was the same as Sadie's—Sinclair. Amy Sinclair.

In the letter, Mrs. Sinclair told the principal that she was enrolling her daughter, enclosing a deposit on the tuition, and having her records sent from Mount Carmel High in Salinas, California. They should arrive any day, she'd added.

But no Carmel High transcripts or other records were in the file, and the letter from Mrs. Sinclair to the school was dated July 18 of this year. There was the usual application form and a copy of the note I had seen in Sadie's possession the other day, notifying her mother of Sadie's advanced placement opportunities.

I pulled out the application and began to scan it. Father was deceased. Mother was employed as a financial consultant? Hmmm . . . the woman I'd seen hadn't looked like any financial consultant. I glanced at the other information on the app, which was pretty standard—dates of vaccinations, previous schools. Nothing jumped out at me. Nothing said, "This is why Sadie is weird and Doug won't talk to you."

Buh-bump. Bump. It was the signal. Kerrie was at the door. I put the folder back in its place, closed and locked the file drawer, and ran to the door to tell Kerrie what I'd found out. Maybe the two of us could make sense of all this.

I turned the knob. Nothing happened. Was it stuck? I tried again. Nothing. The lock held fast.

"Kerrie," I whispered through the door.

"What?" she whispered back.

"It—won't—open," I said, the situation slowly sinking in. Our school had been built in 1933. It was in excellent condition because the administrators were constantly upgrading facilities. Just last year, there had been a big campaign to "enhance security." That included nifty new locks on the office door. I remember reading about it in the newsletter sent to parents once a month. Now I knew what exactly was so secure about these locks. They required a key—on *either* side of the door.

"Do you still have the key?" I asked, already knowing the answer.

"No! I gave it back to Mrs. Williston," she said, sounding panicky.

"Well, go back . . . that's it," I said and hastily added, "that's the plan. Go back and tell Williston you forgot something. You forgot your purse."

"I have my purse!"

"Well, leave it here. Hide it in the bathroom. Tell her you accidentally left it in the office when you picked up the application. Hurry up, Kerrie. They won't be rehearsing all day!"

I heard her running off down the hall. It seemed like an eternity before she returned. And when she did, I noticed something odd about the footsteps. There were too many of them. As they came closer, I heard Kerrie speaking in a strangely loud and high-pitched voice.

"Thank you, *Miss Williston*," she practically shouted in my direction, "for coming up here *with me to unlock the door*. I'm sure I left it in there." Kerrie sounded as if she was practicing for an elocution class, her diction was so fierce and her voice so strong.

"No trouble, dear," Miss Williston said, although she sounded extremely put out.

I ran behind the counter then, decided that was too out in the open, and quickly scooted farther behind the desk, knocking over a trash bin in the process. It fell with a muted clunk. Kerrie must have heard it and started coughing.

"You better get that checked," Miss Williston said as she unlocked the door. "You don't want to infect the entire cast, now do you?" I heard the door swing open and their steps entering the room. I murmured a silent prayer to keep them on the other side of the counter. Fast thinking Kerrie jumped in to save the day.

"Oh my goodness!" she cried. "It's not here. And you know what? I remember now. I left it in the bathroom! Oh, I'm so sorry, Miss Williston. I didn't mean to hold you up."

"Well, come on and get it and I'll walk you out. Do you have someone picking you up?" Miss Williston asked her. Their voices became farther away as they walked to the door, closed it (I heard the lock tumbling shut), and walked away.

"My father. I have to call him. He gave me his *cell phone!* Only a few people know the *number*," she said and proceeded to shout it out for me to hear. Miss Williston must have thought she was nuts.

A few seconds later, I crawled out of my hiding place and sat at the desk. I dialed the number Kerrie had conveniently screamed down the hallway for me, and she picked up after one ring.

"Thank God!" she said when she heard my voice. "I didn't know what else to do. I thought Williston would just give me the key again, but she was finished. Everybody had left. She was the only one there and she insisted on walking me up and . . ."

"Be quiet, Kerrie, and listen. Have you called your dad yet?"

"Yes, I had to. Williston wouldn't leave until she made sure I was okay. I thought she was going to wait here with me, but I told her my father would be here in ten minutes."

"Well, you can't tell your father about this," I said emphatically. "He's a lawyer. He might turn us in or something!"

"Oh, Bianca," Kerrie said, sounding like she was going to cry. "What are we going to do?"

"You're going to have to go home. Call my sister when you get there. Call her on her cell phone and ask her if she's heard from me. If she hasn't, tell her I accidentally got locked in and I need her help." I gave Kerrie Connie's cell phone number.

"What are you going to do?" Kerrie whimpered.

"I'm going to call Con and get her to get her muscle man to help me out again. But just in case I don't get her, you're my backup. You keep trying her until you reach her, okay? I don't want to use this phone too much." For all I knew, the school's phone records would chronicle my calls. No future in that.

"Okay . . ." she said. She rang off reluctantly after I explained it was better if we didn't hang on the phone until her father got there. I was going to try to reach Connie, which I did on the first try, probably while Kerrie was still waiting for her ride.

"Yo, sis," Connie said to me when she heard my voice. "What's this with always calling me on my cell phone?"

"Is the home phone free?"

"Well, no."

I sighed, and explained in barest detail my predicament. I didn't tell her I had maneuvered myself into the office with a purpose. I made it sound like we genuinely had gone in search of the PSAT apps and I accidentally got left behind. I don't know if Connie bought it. All I know is she agreed to help.

"I owe you one," Connie said. "I'll get right out there."

"There might be an alarm on the school grounds, Con. I don't want you setting off any alarms."

"Okay. I'll bring Kurt." She was about to hang up when she came back on the line. "Oh, I forgot— Doug called."

My heart leapt with joy . . . then sank like a stone when she gave me the rest of the message.

"He said if you were back in time, he was going to the seven o'clock show and he could meet you there."

It was now nearly five-thirty. If Connie and Kurt arrived at the school in twenty minutes and took only ten minutes to free me, I would have just enough time to rush home, change, and hop a ride to the theater.

It was impossible. I knew it would take longer than a half hour to get me out of this predicament, and I'd be late for sure for my Doug date—again.

As it turned out, it took three hours. Kurt was tied up and couldn't get away until six o'clock. He and Connie didn't arrive at the school until six-thirty, and it took another hour and a half for Kurt to size up the alarm system and feel confident that he was getting past it and any surveillance cameras without leaving a mark.

They didn't arrive outside the office door until close to seven-thirty. I was frantic by then, despite a few desperate calls to Connie's cell phone to make sure my escape was in progress. Kurt uttered some creative oaths while he worked on the lock, alternately cursing and praising the workmanship on the device. Finally, after a half hour of jiggling and scratching, the door came open.

"I have to pee," I said, running past my sister and Rent-A-Hunk.

When I came out of the bathroom a few minutes later, Connie offered to take me to the theater to meet Doug, but it was past eight. The movie would be over by the time I got there. And maybe he wouldn't even be there. Maybe he looked around for me, didn't see me, and decided I was a total wash-out in the potential girlfriend area.

Kurt gave us a hearty good-bye at the curb before getting into his beat-up Jeep. Connie thanked him and scooted into her car, unlocking the passenger side door for me. When I got in, she turned to me.

"Where to? Want a cheeseburger?"

I realized I hadn't eaten anything since lunch, and that had been a quick bite.

"Okay," I said, dejected.

Cheeseburgers and milkshakes were fast becoming the Doug Consolation Prize. I didn't win the showcase, but I got these nice gifts instead.

Chapter Eleven

Connie took me to Fast Mickey's, a tavern in Highlandtown that was a hangout for off-duty cops. Connie liked it there because it reminded her of our father. Although I hadn't known Dad at all because I was too young when he died, Connie told me about him from time to time. The picture she painted of him made me really regret not being able to know him.

Mom, on the other hand, didn't talk much about him except to occasionally say things like "Your father was a good man." I think one of the reasons Connie went into detective work in the first place was to follow in his footsteps.

Anyway, Connie was most likely to talk about Dad at places like Fast Mickey's. Several guys seemed to know her and there was an air of warm camaraderie in the room, not to mention terrific fried onion rings that were one inch thick and light as air. We ordered some, along with burgers. When they arrived, she began her lecture.

"You know," she said, looking down at her fingers on the polished wooden booth table, "if Dad were here, he would have had your hide for what you did."

"What do mean, what I did?"

She looked up at me and took on what she thought was the gaze of a stern parent. Because she was the oldest, she sometimes thought it was her job to act as Mom's partner in raising us.

"If someone had caught you in that office, it would have been awfully hard to explain how you got locked in."

"Well, it was like this . . ." I began, but she cut me off by holding up her hand.

"Don't make something up. I'd rather not know. Just think about the possible consequences, okay? How disappointed your mother would be, for one."

Ouch. Guilt trip. I resisted the urge to fling sarcastic remarks back at Connie about how she herself was no paragon of fulfilled expectations as far as Mom was concerned. But that would have been too mean. Connie was doing her best.

And then I had one of those little revelations that sometimes light up your brain like the cartoon light bulbs over comic strip characters who have bright ideas. Mom didn't want Connie to be a PI because she was afraid Connie would suffer the same fate as Dad. And maybe she had wanted Dad to be something more, as well.

I shifted in my seat, mumbled a grumpy, "Oh. Well," that I hoped would pass for something of an apology, and began talking about Sadie, eager to change the subject away from my transgressions.

Without revealing my subterfuge for gaining access to the school office, I told my sister all I had learned about Sadie so far.

Sadie was supposedly only fifteen, yet she was driving alone. Her school transcripts had never arrived from California. She drove a car with California plates. And, I was beginning to think her mother was not Lemming Lady.

"Let's go through it fact by fact," Connie said, sipping on her own strawberry shake while I polished off a chocolate one. (I don't understand strawberry shakes. I mean, why drink a shake if it's not a chocolate one? Why do they make those other flavors anyway?) "No speculation. Just the facts."

"Okay," I said. "Sadie Sinclair is new at St. John's this year. She's strange."

"Stick to the facts," said Connie. "Forget opinion. She's new to school this year. She somehow knows the two people we met last week. One of them claims to be her mother. They both accompany her to a bank where she makes a withdrawal. She drives a car. What did her application say for birth date?" Connie stared at me. I had told her about my foray into the files, but I had made it sound like the filing cabinet was left unlocked and the file folder had jumped into my lap like some kind of dancing fish.

"I don't know. Let me think." I closed my eyes and visualized the application. I spit out the date of birth triumphantly, the image coming back to me. The year was consistent with a fifteen-year-old. And then another image came to me, a row of neat numbers, her Social Security number. But something was odd about it, something I couldn't put my finger on.

"What?" Connie asked as I continued to squinch up my eyes. "Why are you making that face? What's bothering you?"

"What was it you told me about Social Security numbers? About that one you said was phony?"

"It had double digit zeroes in the group number. Never done," Connie said, slurping the last of her shake from the bottom of the glass.

That was it! Sadie's number had the same mistake. I told Connie.

"Okay," Connie summed up, "we know she has a Social Security number on her app that doesn't exist. *And* she drives, so it would make sense that maybe she faked her date of birth somewhere along the line too. And, her apartment, I couldn't see all of it, of course . . ."

"What about it?" I asked, feeling like we were getting close to something, but I didn't know what.

"It was awfully bare. No furniture that I could see in the living room. Just one pole lamp. And the room to the right of the door looked bare, too."

"She's living in an empty apartment?"

"Maybe she's living by herself."

"What do you mean?" I asked Connie.

"Maybe she's a runaway," Connie said. "All I could find on the condo is that it belongs to a Mister Ryan Greavey. Greavey was convicted of drug dealing last year. He's in prison."

"Drug dealing? Oh my God!"

"Hold your horses," Connie said. "That doesn't mean anything. Greavey, or whoever is managing his stuff, could have just sub-let the place. It doesn't tell us much. Give me that license number you memorized. I have a friend in Motor Vehicles. She might be able to get me something on a California plate if I tell her Kurt was asking about her." She winked at me.

"Don't forget—Sadie also asked about being framed for murder. And she called you about it," I volunteered.

"She didn't call me. Somebody else did, remember?" Connie said. "But it could have been her just giving a fake name."

Of course it had been, but I couldn't reveal that I knew my sister's voice-mail password, so I shut up about that. "Did this friend ever call again?" I asked instead.

"No. Never did. Maybe the threat evaporated."

"If she's a runaway, Connie, how does she support herself?" I ate the last of the fries.

"She looked like she had more than enough money if she was able to give some to that woman and guy," Connie said.

"Maybe she's in trouble with the law." I sucked in my shake. We lapsed into silence for a few seconds.

"If she calls again," I said, then corrected myself, "if her friend calls again, maybe you could kind of point her in the right direction. Kerrie's dad is a lawyer, you know."

"Yeah, I know."

Later, after Connie had paid the bill and we were at a stop light on our way home, she turned to me and became very stern again. "Don't forget what I said, Bianca, about your little excursion into the school office. This isn't a game, you know."

* * *

Two good things happened the next day. I talked to Doug on the phone and I figured out what to wear to Kerrie's Halloween costume party.

I called Doug right after church when my family was settling into its Sunday veg-out routine. He answered right away and, in contrast to last week's surly mood, sounded happy to hear from me. I explained that I didn't get his Saturday message until too late, and he seemed more than willing to buy that explanation. After all, he shared a voice-mail system with a brother, and probably had many messages of his own slip through the cracks.

I asked if he would be at Kerrie's Halloween party. When he said yes, we talked for nearly twenty minutes about what he should go as. He wasn't too keen on dressing up. But I knew Kerrie would be miserably disappointed if only the girls dressed up. I threw several suggestions at him, each easier than the next, and he found a reason to nix each one.

Grim Reaper? No, he wasn't going to wear a "dress." Zorro? Too childish. Alien? Might require makeup.

"Well, what about an FBI agent? All you'll need is a jacket, sunglasses, and an ID. I can download one off the Internet and laminate it for you."

That did the trick and I went to bed that night feeling like a Chinese menu selection—Double Happiness. Doug and I were friendly again. And I had done my friend Kerrie a favor by convincing Doug to wear a costume to her party.

On Monday, Connie talked to her friend at the Motor Vehicle Administration. But she didn't volunteer the information she had found. I had to drag it out of her.

Okay, okay. I just had to ask her. After the dinner dishes were washed and Mom thought I was doing my homework, I wandered into Connie's lair and popped the question.

"What did you find out about Sadie's license?"

Connie was sitting in a reading chair under a bright light. She had some papers on her lap that she closed in a manila folder when I came in.

"The car belonged to Melinda McEvoy," Connie said.

"So it's stolen?" I asked, already feeling betrayed. I had tried to help Sadie and she was a felon?

"Not that I can tell," Connie said. "That's the odd thing. I did some more checking. Melinda McEvoy is dead."

My mouth fell open to the floor. Well, not really. But I was shocked. Sadie had originally entered my orbit by asking a question about being framed for murder. Now I find out she's driving around in a car that belongs to a dead woman?

"Do you know anything else?" I asked after swallowing hard.

"No. Not much. Only that this Melinda person lived near Monterey, and she died in the spring of this year."

"Sadie transferred in July. That's what it said on her application."

"Okay," Connie said, and then went silent and deep.

"Well, what do you think?"

"I don't know, Bianca. I've learned not to jump to wild conclusions."

"But Sadie could be involved in . . . Well, don't you remember? She called you, asking about being framed for murder. And now . . ."

"A friend of hers called."

"No! It was Sadie," I said emphatically. "You know it was."

Connie looked down, which told me I was right. She knew that the "friend" who had called her was really Sadie.

"Maybe you should contact her," I suggested.

"And say what?"

"Tell her you remember someone calling about being framed for murder and you remember me mentioning her question about that same subject and thought she might want advice. I don't know, offer her some kind of 'buy one, get one free' PI coupon or something."

"What you're suggesting," Connie said slowly and condescendingly, "is that Melinda McEvoy, whoever she is, was murdered and that Sadie is being framed for it."

"Think about it! Lemming Lady and Ice Man get her to withdraw money. They're probably blackmailing her."

"Who is Lemming Lady?"

"The woman at Sadie's apartment. And the man," I said, exasperated. It all seemed so clear to me now. Why couldn't Connie see it too?

"Before you start jumping into La-La Land, I think we need to do a little more digging," Connie said.

"Okay. Like what kind?"

"Like let's find out how Melinda McEvoy died.

That's a start. I can get on it in the morning." She opened her file again and began reading, a clear sign she was finished with me *and* this strategy session.

But I wasn't finished. This PI business was beginning to float my boat. Although I was a good student, and got great comments on most of my papers, I was completely clueless as to what I wanted to do with my life. As things stood now, I was on the fast track to a stellar career in the "Undeclared Major" department of any decent university.

Working on the Sadie case, however, was presenting me with a focused challenge. Maybe I'd follow in Connie's footsteps after all. Then again, maybe I'd become a trial lawyer, and then a top prosecutor, and then an Attorney General, and then, heck—why not dream big?—a Supreme Court Justice. Nothing seemed out of reach now that I had a mission.

I went downstairs to the kitchen and logged on to the Internet. As soon as I was online, a chirpy IM from Kerrie appeared. I filled her in about Doug's costume—which I hadn't had a chance to do during school that day—and told her I was working on a paper. She chirped back with a question about what I was going to wear. "A shroud," I retorted, but added a smiling emoticon so she'd know I wasn't being irritable, even though I was.

While we bantered back and forth, I pulled up a search program and plugged in Melinda McEvoy's name. Zero documents retrieved, and the same non-results came up over and over. I tried just the last name and got the exact opposite result—thousands upon thousands of possible entries ranging from

McEvoy Bed and Breakfast in Lowell, Massachusetts to the McEvoy family tree in Dust Ridge, Kentucky.

On and on I went, trying M. McEvoy and even looking through the Internet white pages in California. Too many McEvoys popped up again, including a few dozen or so in the Monterey area. I actually thought of copying these names and numbers down and trying a few, but with nothing more to go on, it seemed too expensive and too frivolous to make all those long-distance calls for what could end up being a wild goose chase.

Besides, what would I say when I called all these M. McEvoys? "Excuse me, aren't you supposed to be dead?"

In the meantime, Kerrie chimed in to say she had found a great old "flapper" costume her mother once had worn to a party. She was sure it would fit me, and if Doug was coming as an FBI agent, he could be Eliot Ness to my Zelda Fitzgerald. I said okay just to make her feel good, figuring the costume probably wouldn't fit me anyway.

Maybe it was mentioning Zelda Fitzgerald, the wife of 1920s novelist F. Scott Fitzgerald, that got me to thinking about writing, and writing got me to thinking about reporting, and reporting got me to thinking about newspapers. Just as I was about to sign off and give up the hunt, I decided to try newspapers in the Monterey area.

I quickly found a couple major dailies and pulled up their web sites. Then, I punched in "Melinda McEvoy" and waited, expecting no result. Well, actually I was hoping for some story on a murder victim by that name. A few seconds later, an obituary appeared.

"McEvoy, Melinda," the notice read, "passed away on May 11." It was an ordinary and very brief obit, nothing jumping off the page to solve the mystery. Melinda McEvoy was forty-five when she died. The obit didn't say what had led to her demise or anything about family.

Had Sadie known the McEvoys? Had she taken their car? Or had Melinda McEvoy given it to her? Connie said the car was not listed as stolen as far as she knew.

It was getting late. One more piece of the puzzle, but still no clear picture in sight.

I had every intention of keeping the McEvoy information to myself while I looked for more to flesh out the story. After all, my goal now was to excel at this investigation business so I could pave my way to more triumphs in the corridors of justice later on.

I wanted to solve this mystery and present the whole thing to Connie wrapped up in a nice big bow, so to speak. Call me crazy, but I had this thing about wanting to show her I could surpass her in the PI department.

My secrecy plan, however, was foiled early the next morning by circumstances beyond my control.

Okay, okay, it was more my lack of *self*-control. I got mad at Connie and spilled the beans.

But she was so darned smug, warming her hands around her mug of herbal tea, reading the newspaper at the kitchen table with eyes half closed while I had already showered and dressed and was ready for school. The kicker, though, was when she asked me if

I wanted to drop by her office to learn more about her filing system.

Her filing system? This was her summer employment offer? I was an experienced sleuth by now. And I wanted Connie to recognize my superior talents.

"Filing?" I asked, withering scorn dripping from my voice.

"Yeah. Filing. As in a part-time job. I thought you wanted to make some extra cash." She casually flipped a page. "I thought you wanted to learn more about the business. We've talked about this."

"Filing isn't learning about the business," I sputtered. "Filing is—putting papers in folders."

"What do you expect to do—bring in serial killers single-handed?" Connie didn't even look at me when she said that. That was what unlocked my sealed lips. Not so much the fact that she wanted me to do grunt-level filing, but that she didn't even look at me when she threw a sarcastic remark my way. This was war.

"For your information," I said icily. "I know who Melinda McEvoy is."

"Huh?" She kept reading the paper, not paying any attention. I smacked my hand on top of what she was reading so she'd have to look at me.

"Melinda McEvoy. You know, the woman whose car Sadie is driving?"

Did Connie kiss my hand? Did she start to exclaim what a clever girl I was? Did she thank me, bless me, offer me the keys to her office? Of course.

Not.

"Let me guess. She died on May 11." Connie stood and put her now-empty mug in the sink. "And you don't know squat about why Sadie has her car. Hmm . . . I think that adds up to a big, fat goose egg in the investigation department. I think it adds up to what I already know."

I answered this with a stinging rebuke—silence.

"Unless the information you found said, 'oh, by the way, Sadie Sinclair is now using Melinda McEvoy's car because . . .' it doesn't tell us much. Besides, I already knew McEvoy was dead, probably from the same on-line obit you read, Sherlock. And I know the car hasn't been reported stolen, so I'm assuming Sadie knew McEvoy well enough to get the car after McEvoy passed on. Not to worry. Unlike you, I've got some other things I can check."

"Like what?"

From upstairs I heard Tony calling me. "You ready to roll, rat head?" he called out in his usual dulcet tones.

"In a minute!" I yelled back, just as sweetly. Standing, I turned my attention back to Connie. "Like what, Connie? What else can you check to find out about Melinda McEvoy and her connection to Sadie?"

Connie said nothing at first but just leaned against the sink, twisting her mouth to one side as if deciding what to reveal and what to keep hidden. I'm not sure if her reasons included an indepth analysis of "need-to-know" requirements. I think it was more along the lines of "if I tell Bianca, will she feel like she won something here?"

Whatever the outcome of her inner debate, it was interrupted by Tony, who flew into the kitchen. Mom had told him the night before he had to take me to school today. She was already at work, putting in extra hours to earn Christmas money.

"Come on, Bianca! I'm going to be late!"

I grabbed my backpack from the kitchen floor and shrugged into my blue blazer. "Well?" I asked Connie one last time.

"I have a few databases I can check, a few friends I can call," she said nonchalantly. "Things and people a PI knows. Internet search engines have their limitations." She turned to the sink and began washing the breakfast dishes.

I harrumphed as best I could and briskly followed Tony to the door.

Chapter Twelve

When I arrived at school, there was little time to stew about Connie's smugness or her secretiveness or her arrogance. Right away, I ran into Kerrie, who proceeded to overwhelm me with her enthusiasm for the flapper costume. She'd brought it with her, neatly folded in a paper grocery bag (Kerrie's family didn't believe in plastic bags), and made me take a look at it in the locker hall before class.

I have to admit I was expecting maybe a slightly better version of a K-Mart costume. You know the kind—thin fabric with designs glued on in sparkles or sequins, maybe a plastic mask thrown in for good measure. This was more like the Neiman Marcus version of that. It was a gorgeous mauve colored silk with real beading and fringe sewn on. It came with a matching cloche hat, purse, shoes, and tons of sparkling jewelry. In fact, this didn't look like a costume at all. It looked like the real thing—something a flapper had actually worn.

"Wow," I said, stretching my descriptive powers to the limit. "This is great."

"I knew you'd like it," Kerrie said. "If the shoes are too big, maybe you can stick tissue in the toes or something."

"Hmm, how should I do my hair?" I reached up and touched it. Today it was pulled back in a scrunchie in a fetchingly uncomplicated "natural" look. In other words, it was a little on the messy side.

"Oh, let me do it for you! Come over early. I have a crimper and a curling iron. Or, you could come in the afternoon and I'll set it in pin curls." Kerrie was practically squealing with joy. And I have to admit that having her do my hair was probably better than trying to do it myself. At least if Kerrie did it, I could blame it on her. And that included blaming it on her if it looked really good.

You have to understand that looking too good, or looking like you try too hard to look good, is just as bad as looking bad. So, having someone else responsible for part of your look was a great way to look good without worrying about looking like you tried hard to look good. You can sort of shrug and say, "Well, Kerrie did it," and everyone would understand that you just *had* to look this good because Kerrie's feelings would be hurt otherwise.

Am I making myself clear here?

"Okay," I agreed. "We can make a plan later."

We parted ways for class, and hardly had a moment the rest of that busy day to catch up. Even the lunch hour was filled with announcements and special activities. Kerrie was starting a Christmas donation fund and stood at the cafeteria mike giving out detailed lists of items she would need to make the project work.

I like Kerrie, but even *I* was rolling my eyes after the thirtieth description of the kind of toys that were *not* acceptable as donations. "Nothing made in China, if you don't mind. Nothing on the Consumer Safety Products Warning List. Nothing made by BonCo Toys because they use child labor in India . . ."

By the time she was done, I felt like running to the mike myself and sobbing to the mesmerized crowd, "I confess, I confess"—quite a few of the forbidden toys were stashed away in my old toy box. My mother hadn't been as enlightened, I guess, when she'd played Santa Claus.

My guilt at inadvertently exploiting the underprivileged played second fiddle to other, more immediate concerns. First off were the encounters with Doug.

Deciding how to react to Doug, how to interpret his reactions, and plotting future encounters with him was beginning to occupy a lot of my time at school. Not that some classes weren't interesting enough to divert me. My history teacher, for example, was one riveting lady who made us all work so hard we forgot we were working hard.

Hmm . . . history would come in handy in my new career path—World Court High Justice (I'd moved up from the Supreme Court, you see.)

Anyway, I saw Doug a few times during the day and once he actually smiled and said, "Kerrie's party!" while pointing his index finger at me. In the shorthand of the day, I was sure he really meant, "I cannot wait until our tryst, my darling beloved."

Kerrie's party, in fact, was beginning to take on mythic importance. It would give me the opportunity to be with Doug, maybe even dance, hold hands (that sent a shiver down my spine), and generally be close. It would make up for those encounters of the fouled-up kind we'd been having. Or not having.

And I also had a kind of electric feeling that something big would happen at the party. Sadie had been invited, and probably was going to come. Thus, there might be opportunities to pry more information out of her, or to observe her or learn something new about her. I wasn't sure how. Maybe someone would show up dressed as a medieval torture chamber operator, and could scare information out of her.

My mind was so full of hope because of Doug that I was beginning to think anything could happen: a revelation from Sadie; an admission of devotion from Doug; a job offer from Kerrie's lawyer father. The possibilities were endless.

Of course, part of my hope for getting info out of Sadie was buoyed by my simmering resentment of Connie. I wanted to show her up, to uncover Sadie's secrets on my own, and make Connie feel bad for offering me anything less than the equivalent of a partnership in her PI agency. It's amazing what an energy boost resentment and anger can provide.

As it turned out, I didn't see my sister much the rest of the week. She was busy on an insurance fraud case, my mother told me on one of the nights Connie's chair was empty at the dinner table. And one night Connie actually had a date—with Kurt of all people. I wondered if my mother had ever seen the guy.

These Connie-less dinners were actually nice occasions to chat with my mom, who was usually pretty frazzled from work. Tony was out a lot that week, too, because of his college and work schedule, so that meant lots of bonding time for me and Mom.

On Thursday night that week, I talked to her about Sadie, explaining how odd she was and how Kerrie and I didn't think she was telling us everything.

My mother grimaced while her fork of macaroni and cheese paused in midair.

"There are a lot of girls who don't have the best home life," she said philosophically. "Have you ever met Sadie's parents?"

I didn't want to tell her about Lemming Lady and Ice Man, so I just said "no." Besides, I really didn't think they were her parents. They wanted something from her all right, but it wasn't a daughter's affection.

"Have you ever seen any signs of trouble, of abuse?" Mom asked. "You know, funny bruises, black eyes, anything like that?

"Heck no," I answered quickly. "If anything, Sadie seems to be alone. Like her parents don't exist."

Mom got even more serious.

"Do you think she could have run away from home?" she asked me.

"Connie thinks that's a possibility. But how could she live on her own at the age of fifteen?" I asked. "How would she support herself?"

My mother didn't answer at first, but ate silently for a few seconds. Then she blurted out her theory.

"What if Sadie was earning money to support herself? Does she have a job?"

"No. No visible means of support."

"Do you think she's into drugs, prostitution?" My

mother peered at me through squinty eyes, obviously concerned that I'd be hanging out with a bad type.

"No!" Methinks I doth protest too much, my inner (Shakespearean) voice declared. I *had*, of course, suspected Sadie of those things. I just hadn't articulated them.

In truth, Sadie's life did not paint a picture of goodness and light. Look at the people around her. The knife-wielding, tough-talking Lemming Lady was no saint. Just thinking of her gave me the creeps. And then there was the condo—owned by a jailed drug dealer. Finally, Ice Man looked as if he had seen his share of trouble and liked it that way.

"How would you know?" my mother asked, and I began to fear we'd soon be treading into dangerous waters.

"Uh, well, you know. Kids talk. You hear things," I said. I stood and took my plate to the sink, scraping the scraps into the garbage disposal.

"If you hear things, you should tell me. You should not let friends engage in dangerous behaviors." Mom, too, stood and did the plate-scraping routine. We loaded the dishwasher together.

She was right, of course, and if I ever saw Kerrie or Nicole doing or saying anything that led me to believe they were headed for trouble, I'd make sure responsible people knew so they could help.

But, despite Sadie's unseemly circle, I sensed in her a desire to be wholesome, as if she might have run away from a seamier life and was trying to start over.

"Do you have homework?" my mother asked. She placed the last dish in the machine, poured detergent in the little compartments, and flipped the thing on.

"A little. I need the computer," I said, improvising. I needed it all right, but to look up more stuff about Sadie Sinclair and Melinda McEvoy. Sure, I had a one-page essay to write, but I could do that pretty quickly.

"Well, I'm going to watch the news." As she went by, Mom gave me a cheery punch in the shoulder and headed for the living room, where she settled in her favorite chair and flicked on the tube. As I heard the sounds of the evening newscast skittering into the room, I plunked myself in front of the computer and got to work.

To my credit (if I do say so myself), I whipped off the one-page essay on "a discussion of internal and external conflicts in the play *Antigone*" first. Then I turned the sound off so as not to disturb my mother, and started up the old Internet engine.

I revved up my imaginative and investigative instincts to a high pitch. Sadie seemed to be running away from something. She had a California car that had belonged to Melinda McEvoy. Had Melinda McEvoy employed her? Abused her? Been her mother?

With lightning speed, I raced through search after search trying to find out if Melinda McEvoy had had any children. Her obit didn't list survivors. I tried plugging in "Sadie McEvoy," "Melinda Sinclair," "Melinda Sadie," any combination I could think of. Nothing.

I tried looking through online archives of newspapers in California searching for a clue, using anything I could think of. But the brick wall I kept running into was this—if Sadie was running from something, chances were she wasn't using her own name.

Chances are she'd faked a lot of stuff, maybe even a driver's license.

After an hour and a half of this, I gave up and disconnected. Checking the voice mail on the phone, I found I had three messages. My heart leapt for joy. Surely one of the messages would be from Doug.

But Tony's cold voice greeted me instead.

"This is Tony. I'm stuck at Burger Boy. My car won't start. Battery's dead. Can you come help me out?"

Next message: "Tony again. I still need a jumpstart. Nobody here has cables."

Final message, five minutes before I got off the Internet: "If that's you on the phone, Bianca, you're gonna pay. I need someone to come get me. For crissake, get off the phone!"

So that Mom would not be disturbed by Tony's cursing, I thoughtfully erased the messages. Then I informed her of his distress.

She immediately jumped up and muttered, "Oh, dear," then ran for her purse and coat.

"I'll be back in an hour or so. Stay off the phone and the Internet in case I need to call you," she said at the door.

After she left, I was all alone. And despite Mom's warning about staying off the phone, I knew that she wouldn't be in a position to use a phone for at least twenty minutes, maybe even more, until she reached Burger Boy.

So, for a brief period of time, I would be in teenage paradise—an empty house and access to the phone. Thinking quickly, I checked the time. It was nearly seven-thirty.

Seven-thirty, *eastern* time. It would be four-thirty on the West Coast. That meant offices there would still be open.

To heck with the Internet, I thought, picking up the receiver. I would go directly to the source. I flipped through the phone book looking for the area code for Sadie's old stomping grounds. Finding it, I punched it in and the number for information. When the mechanical voice came on asking me what I was after, I blurted out, "Department of Social Services."

This was vague enough to get a real live operator on the line who helped me navigate through some governmental listings until I had a couple phone numbers for various branch offices of social services.

It was now seven-forty. I figured offices closed at five, which would be eight o'clock our time. Plus, Mom would be at Burger Boy by then and if she tried to call me, I'd be dead meat when she got voice mail. (Of course, I could always tell her a telephone solicitor called me, tying up the line for ungodly amounts of time. I was good at improvising preemptive excuses.) Anyway, I had about twenty minutes.

Deadlines are good for yours truly. Deadlines make me think. Deadlines make me smarter.

In my limited time, what information did I want the most? I already knew that asking about Sadie Sinclair was likely to lead nowhere. By now I was convinced that Sadie Sinclair was an alias. In fact, I was beginning to think that Sadie had plucked it out of the air after seeing promotional material for the artist Sadie Mauvais Sinclair.

She'd probably figured no one in their right mind would ever track down the connection. (Please do not insert a sarcastic thought here about whether I am in my right mind. My ego, after all, is no less fragile than your own!)

No, if I wanted to find something, I would have to stick to real people and real names. And the only real name I had was Melinda McEvoy's.

I dialed the number while mentally racing down a list of excuses I could use to find out more about the recently deceased McEvoy. As the phone rang and rang, my pulse pounded. Think, Bianca, think.

A disembodied voice came on the line, asking me if I needed help.

"Uh, yes, I, er, need to find out some information about Melinda McEvoy," I said. Brilliant, Bianca, I thought to myself. What imagination!

When the woman justifiably asked for more info— like just what I needed to find out and who Melinda McEvoy is, my brain finally got a jolt of Creativity Plus.

"I'm calling on behalf of Lifetime Insurance," I said, my voice becoming stronger now that the charade came to me. "Ms. McEvoy had a policy worth five-hundred-thousand dollars. I understand she's passed away and I'm trying to find her daughter, who is listed as the beneficiary. I thought her daughter might be a ward of the state now."

How *did* I come up with this stuff? I have no idea. It popped into my mind as if some cartoonist were drawing dialogue balloons right over my head. I just knew that Melinda and Sadie were connected and that if Melinda passed away, maybe Sadie was running away from the fate that awaited her in foster care.

I was put on hold. I fretted. I sweated. I looked at the clock. I worried what my mother would say if and when she saw this long-distance call on the phone bill. Luckily, I'd have a few weeks to make up that explanation. I wondered if there was something illegal about pretending to be an insurance representative. Maybe fraud investigators were tracing my call right now.

It was seven-fifty-three. My finger hovered over the switch-hook, ready to end this call before I was apprehended, before Mom tried to call home.

Then, eureka! Success! Beyond my wildest dreams!

"This is Mrs. Santos," a woman said. "I understand you're looking for Melinda McEvoy's daughter. According to our records, Sarah McEvoy turned eighteen right after her mother died, so we have no more jurisdiction over her. But the last address we have is one in Salinas. I can give you that."

With a trembling hand, I wrote it down. It was familiar. Where had I seen it before? It was the same as the return address on Sadie's school file letter—the letter supposedly written by her mother explaining her transfer to St. John's.

Sadie was Melinda McEvoy's daughter. Her real name was Sarah McEvoy. And she wasn't fifteen.

Chapter Thirteen

When I figured out that Sadie Sinclair was really Sarah McEvoy, I felt like I'd discovered gold. I wanted to rush out and tell everyone what I knew, but at the same time I wanted to keep it quiet in case someone would elbow in on my territory.

Actually, the "someone" I most had in mind was Connie. Finding this information before she did was a real coup, one that showed I knew my stuff and was overqualified for a lowly file-clerk position in her office. If I just handed the info over to Connie, however, she most likely would take it and run with it and leave me in file-clerk land. By the time I was done, I wanted her to offer me an equal partnership.

But, full to bursting with this tidbit, it was all I could do to keep from spitting it out when Mom returned home with a very disgruntled Tony forty minutes later.

"Bianca," my mother said in a tired voice after she threw her keys on the half-table by the door. "Tony says he tried calling several times but you were on the phone."

Tony, who was in the kitchen by now swigging a bottle of juice, chimed in.

"Yeah. I must have tried five times and got the voice mail each time."

"You did not try five times!" He had left only three messages.

"Did too, punk. Didn't leave a message each time."

Mom stepped in. "Don't call your sister names, Tony. I'll deal with it."

Tony stood waiting to witness my execution, but Mom told him to go upstairs to work on school stuff. Then she sat at the kitchen table and looked as stern as Connie had tried to look the night she lectured me in Fast Mickey's.

"Bianca, I can't afford a second phone line right now. So that means we all have to be considerate. I had no idea you were on the computer so long or I would have told you to get off."

"Maybe I can get a job," I said, thinking of my new investigative skills and how valuable they'd be to Connie once I solved the Sadie mystery completely. "And I can pay for the second line."

"It's a monthly fee," my mother continued. "It's not a one-time expense."

"Well, maybe I can still chip in . . ." I petered out, not sure I wanted to commit to a long-running debt.

"I'm afraid I'm going to have to make a rule," she said. "No tying up the phone for more than a half hour at a time."

That smarted. Of course I wondered about the sub-sections of this new law. Like, was there a paragraph in there that said "whereas if half-hour sessions are interrupted by sessions off the phone that are at least five minutes in duration, unlimited half-hour sessions on the phone may be scheduled"? I wasn't sure. But I *was* sure this was not a good time to ask.

And, just as obviously, it wasn't a good time to get on the phone, either. So my plan to reveal my Sadie info to Kerrie just flew out the window. But it made me take some time to think through what I knew and how I could use it.

I went up to my room and did just that. I dug through the pile of papers on my desk and found an old notebook that I'd hardly used. After ripping out the pages with old history essays, I started writing down what I knew:

- *Sadie Sinclair is Sarah McEvoy*
- *Sarah McEvoy is eighteen years old.*
- *Sadie/Sarah is a whiz at computers and knows something about music.*
- *Sadie/Sarah worries she might be framed for murder.*
- *Sadie/Sarah is being pursued by Lemming Lady and Ice Man.*
- *Lemming Lady claims to be Sadie's mother. Sadie affirmed her motherhood. But both are lying.*
- *Sadie has given money to Lemming Lady and Ice Man.*
- *Sadie's real mother was Melinda McEvoy, who passed away this spring.*

What haunted me most about the whole list was the final factoid. Sadie's mom had died in the spring, and, from the sound of the social worker in California, it didn't look like Sadie had a dad. That meant she was all alone, thrown out into the world at the age of seventeen, then legally on her own just a short time later after turning eighteen. I flipped my notebook shut and ran downstairs.

My mother was watching television, but she muted it when I came in the room and a commercial started to air.

"Mom, what happens to kids in foster care when they turn eighteen?" I plopped into an arm chair, my legs sprawled over the arm.

"That's a tough one. Once a kid turns eighteen, they're legally considered an adult. I know of kids who were in the foster system all their lives, then were completely left to their own devices just a few months from high school graduation. It's very sad." She looked at me quizzically. "Why do you want to know?"

"No reason. Just a paper I was thinking of writing." When she turned her gaze to my legs, I shimmied around and sat up straight. "But how do those kids survive? Do they get jobs?"

"Most have to work to survive, which means they drop out of school. A few organizations are springing up to help solve the problem. There's a shelter downtown for high school kids who turn eighteen and get tossed out of 'the system.' I understand they're doing some wonderful work, even helping kids get into college and find scholarships. Do you want me to bring you some information on it?"

"Sure. That would be great," I said.

The show Mom was watching started flickering back on the screen, so I shut up and let her unmute the thing. After a few seconds watching some deadly dull animal show, I ran back upstairs.

Opening my notebook, I added one new observation to my list. Sadie lives alone, but has money. Where does she get it?

Musing on this problem the rest of the evening, I downed a bowl of peanut butter fudge ice cream and some microwave popcorn. Tony stayed secluded in his room the whole night, Connie was still out, and Mom was watching her diet as well as TV, which left the refrigerator-grazing all to me.

As I wandered in and out of the kitchen, the siren call of the computer beckoned. I considered getting online for the permissible half hour. Mom was engrossed in her show, right? But I figured that would be pushing it, and I didn't want to irritate Mom.

Back upstairs, I thought so much that, to keep my brain from exploding, I found myself forced to actually clean up my room. But as I hung up clothes, and threw away old papers, an idea began to take hold.

Lemming Lady and Ice Man had something on Sadie. They were the ones who got money from her. And they were the ones who probably had threatened to frame her for murder. What was it they knew that Sadie didn't want known? My guess was it had something to do with the way she earned her money.

When I woke up the next morning, it was raining, a gray, steady curtain of rain. Tony was still mad at me, and Mom had arranged for Connie to drive me to school, probably in an attempt to keep familial harmony.

Connie was being nice to me that morning, which

made it easier to keep to myself the secret of Sadie's true identity. If Connie had acted like a jerk, I might have been forced to reveal the info as a sort of missile defense shield—something sent into the atmosphere to knock out incoming, ego-bursting projectiles.

As she drove me into school, Connie asked me about my Halloween costume and seemed genuinely interested in my dress and hair plans. One date with Kurt had sure put her in a good mood. Come to think of it, he *was* a hunky guy.

At school, I looked eagerly for Kerrie but didn't see her in the locker hall. But when I caught a glimpse of her outside French class, I could have sworn she was getting ready to audition for the part of an extra on "Night of the Living Dead." Her face was pallid, and her eyes looked red.

I didn't find out why until lunchtime, when I managed to rush into the cafeteria and snag two prime private seats in the far corner by the auditorium doorway. Kerrie caught sight of my cheery wave as soon as she entered, and headed my way.

"What's up with *you?*" I asked, foraging through my change purse for milk money. "You looked awful this morning."

"Thanks a lot, Bianca." She threw her books down on the table with a plop. "It's this rain."

"Everybody gets a little down in the rain. But it's been really dry. We need it."

"Well, I wish we could have another dry weekend. This rain is going to ruin my party! I was planning on putting up lanterns in the backyard and all."

Now I know it probably sounds really superficial for Kerrie to be so upset about the weather affecting her party when the rain was probably helping farmers, but you have to understand my friend. She's a planner. She plans things so thoroughly that she makes lists of the lists she has to make to get things done.

So when something as crude as the weather throws a monkey wrench into things, I can understand her feeling that maybe she's being singled out by some unseen spirit bent on spiting her for her great planning abilities. She takes it personally.

"First of all, Kerrie, I think it's supposed to stop raining tonight," I offered. "And secondly, you've got a great house and, if it rains, we can do something special inside. Let me get my milk and we can start making some plans. Why don't you make a list of the outdoor decorations you bought?"

Am I good or what? As soon as I uttered the magic words—"list" and "plans"—Kerrie immediately started to lose her waif-like countenance. By the time I returned to the table with my milk, she was bright-eyed, already halfway through her list and full of plans for how to turn the outdoor theme into an indoor extravaganza.

"You know, this could actually work out better," she said, scanning her notes. "All this stuff inside could be really festive."

"Disaster ahead," my inner alarm system screamed. If the rain stopped, Kerrie might be thrown into the dumps again, torn by two great, conflicting plans. Time to step in.

"Both ways would be really festive. So whatever happens, you're golden." Like I said, I'm good.

I got so caught up in the party-planning comforting thing that I didn't spill the beans about Sadie.

I know, I know—it's hard to imagine how I, Bianca "Tell-It-Now" Balducci, could keep a secret. But not being able to use the phone the night before had changed me. I was more serene, more peaceful, less frantic.

Actually, I think I was going through withdrawal.

Anyhoo, the day passed and still only I (and Sadie, of course) knew Sadie's real identity. The only time I came close to letting it loose was at the end of the day, when I saw Sadie herself. She smiled at me and said "I'll see you at the party" in such a hopeful, happy way that I felt guilty for knowing she wasn't who she said she was. She didn't look devious or mean or criminal. She just looked like a girl trying to work things out. She looked like someone trying to lead a better, more normal life.

Uh-oh. Moral dilemma. As I rode the bus home that afternoon, it occurred to me that by uncovering Sadie's secrets, I could be jeopardizing her happiness. If she was involved in something a little on the sad side of ethical, I could land her in a heap of hurt by finding out what it was.

Suddenly, my investigative prowess didn't seem so sweet anymore. In fact, it kind of left a bitter taste in my mouth.

Chapter Fourteen

As I had predicted to Kerrie the day before, Saturday dawned sunny and beautiful. No rain, just cool air, and a few unthreatening clouds dancing across the sky. What more could she ask for?

My guess was that any puddles in her backyard would be dried by party time. And if they weren't, I was sure she'd convince her dad to rent some water-sucking device to dry them up. Or Kerrie would build one herself to do the job.

She called me three times that morning to go over last-minute plans, and two times that afternoon. Well aware of my family's new "half-hour" rule, I carefully noted how much time I spent with Kerrie each time she called.

Luckily, Kerrie was in such a hurry to make sure everything was just right that she didn't want to talk long. I was never in danger of violating the rule, which gave me great satisfaction the times Tony wandered into the kitchen shortly after the phone had rung for me and I was already off.

In fact, I strongly suspect he came into the kitchen on at least two occasions solely to see if I was still on the phone. It breaks my heart thinking of all those unused reprimands stored in his brain.

Well, not really.

In one of our phone connections, Kerrie and I planned to meet at her place around three so she could help me with my hair and I could help her finish decorating. I'd already planned to meet Doug at the party, thus avoiding the awkward "who drives us?" scenario, so all I needed to do was get one of my siblings to take me over at the appointed hour.

Tony was hanging out most of the day, which was odd because he was usually so busy. But he did get one Saturday a month off at Burger Boy and he'd just finished some big paper for an econ class. So he was multitasking in the living room—napping and watching TV.

Mom, on the other hand, was a virtual whirlwind of cheerful activity. She'd gone to the grocery store in the morning and baked a cake after lunch, then tried to entice me into helping her sew, but I managed to beg off. Still, it was nice hearing her hum as she laid out the green velvet fabric on the kitchen table.

Connie, I decided, was my best bet for chauffeuring duty. She'd been off the hook a lot this week because of work and Kurt, and I still had this sense that she owed me something because of her previous snide remarks about my investigative skills. Funny how something like that can stick in my craw when so many things that Tony does just roll off my back. It must be a girl thing.

In the morning, Connie had gone to her office, but

was back by lunchtime and in her room in the afternoon. I waltzed in there a little after noon and gave her the directive.

"You're taking me to Kerrie's at three, right?" I said without wavering. I found it was best to present these things as givens, as if they'd been discussed and agreed to in some previous conversation. Sometimes, Tony, Mom, or Connie would just look at me funny and say "Yeah, I guess" as they tried to remember when they'd made the commitment.

Connie, however, was getting harder to fool.

"I wish you would have asked me earlier. I would have gone into work this afternoon instead of this morning and just dropped you off on the way." Connie was sitting in her chair leafing through some thick file. A notebook was balanced on one knee, and several videotapes were on the table beside her.

"You working on something?" I asked, pointing to the tapes and notes.

"Just finishing up my report on an insurance fraud case," she said.

"How do you do that?"

She sighed heavily, and looked put upon. "It's pretty simple, really," she said. Then, warming to her topic, she leaned forward and explained: "Every PI does it a little differently. I like to break it down into several components. I write a nice, short cover letter to the client that summarizes in a few quick sentences whether we met the investigative goals."

"What do you mean?"

"Well, if the client wants us to see if someone is bilking them out of insurance money, I write that down and then say yes, we were able to determine

149

that so-and-so is engaging in what appears to be fraudulent behavior, or no, we did not observe any, or the information we found and the observations we made are inconclusive. Then I write a quick boilerplate sentence or two about the techniques. Then I refer them to the enclosed report."

"And what's in that?"

"I outline how we did the investigation—records looked into, surveillance, interviews. All that stuff. But I keep it nice and readable. Like a story. I save the times, dates, and other data for the appendix at the end. Then I do a section called 'Findings' where I list our observations and, well, findings. Then I do a 'Conclusions' section where I tie it all together. Sometimes I even include a 'Recommendations' section where I might recommend they take a case to the police or alter a security procedure or something. Then there's the appendix with the supporting documentation."

"Wow. That sounds like a lot of work." I was starting to reassess whether being a private investigator was worth all the effort. Maybe I could leapfrog over it to High Court Justice.

"It's not all Nancy Drew skulking-around, you know. It's methodical, painstaking. It's not glamorous."

"Who's Nancy Drew?"

Connie threw me a look but I swerved to avoid it.

"I haven't had a chance to follow up on your friend, by the way," Connie continued. "Maybe next week if I have a little extra time. I've been busy."

"Yeah. With Kurt." Bull's-eye. Connie blushed.

"Kurt's a friend."

"Uh-huh. Hear ya. Anyhoo, can we leave around two-thirty?"

"It only takes five minutes to get to Kerrie's, Bianca."

"It takes longer than that."

"Well, not a half hour."

"I want to be early. To help Kerrie."

"You're already going early." Connie sighed again and shook her head. "But okay. Two-thirty. I'll take you. Who's picking you up?"

"Not sure. I might be able to get a ride."

"Just let Mom know so she doesn't worry, okay?"

"Okay."

At exactly two-thirty, I was knocking on Connie's bedroom door, a canvas tote bag under my arm. In it was the flapper costume, my makeup bag, some perfume, and other assorted items I would need to create the alluring image I was after. Or just to look decent.

Connie, car keys in hand, appeared without a word, and we headed off after a quick farewell to Mom, who was now in the kitchen making chicken soup from scratch. The smell of it made me hungry and I hoped Kerrie had a meal break planned in the afternoon's festivities.

On the way to Kerrie's, Connie decided to be sisterly and started chatting me up about my life, Doug, schoolwork, you name it. Finally, she came to Sadie.

"I've been thinking about your friend, Bianca. You should consider confronting her with what you know and urging her to get help if she needs it. After all, what's the point of figuring out her problem except to get her help? You can do that without having all the pieces to the puzzle."

I felt like hitting myself in the head with the flat of

my hand. Actually, hitting Connie in the head with my hand would have been a whole lot more satisfying, but what I mean is that Connie had indeed made an important observation, one that I had conveniently shoved out of my mind as I focused on the party, Kerrie, and seeing Doug.

Why in the heck was I trying to figure out Sadie's secrets? Just so I could say I'd done it? Just so I could wave it under Connie's nose and hear her admit I was a phenomenal investigator with superior intellectual skills?

As a matter of fact, I'd envisioned just such a scenario a couple of times since finding out Sadie's real identity. My favorite one was where I came to Connie's office just as she was in the midst of a meeting with an Important Client. I'd be dressed all in black, maybe some black stretch pants and leather jacket, boots, hair kind of spiky. I'd look really tough, cool, and smart.

Connie would interrupt the meeting to hear what I had to say (okay, so I hadn't figured out why she'd interrupt the meeting). I would present my findings, maybe even slap a three-inch-thick report on her desk (I'd added this detail just today after hearing about how she writes up her own reports), and give an oral presentation of such sweeping grace and rhetorical clarity that her jaw would actually hang open. And so would the mouth of the Important Client. Oh, yeah, and Kurt's mouth would open, too. I just thought of that—Kurt being there.

So all three of them would be staring at me wonder-struck. And Connie would swallow hard and say, "Bianca, that's pretty impressive." And the Important Client would say, "Would you assign her to my case?" And Kurt would say (with a smile and a wink), "You better sign her up right away, Con. And don't give her any filing jobs. This girl's headed for an appointment with destiny."

Okay, so that wasn't exactly Kurt's style, but this is, after all, *my* fantasy.

Those images were now sucked out of my brain by the vacuum of Ethical Dilemma. How many ethical dilemmas can one girl handle in such a short time, huh? What was going on here?

My dilemma was—do I solve the mystery or do I help Sadie? Sure, they weren't mutually exclusive, but helping Sadie could occur without solving her mystery.

The point was, if I waited until I had all the "pieces of the puzzle," as Connie put it, and if Sadie was truly in trouble, I might be jeopardizing her safety. Why not turn my recently discovered investigative skills into superior powers of persuasion? If I could figure out who Sadie was, surely I could convince her to come clean and go to the authorities if she was in trouble. Right?

"That's a good idea," I said to Connie. I was feeling so generous of spirit now that my thoughts were focused on what should be the endgame—helping Sadie—that I finally spilled the beans.

But hey, this had to be a record—thirty-eight and a half hours since I'd uncovered Sadie's identity. Nearly forty hours! And I hadn't told a soul. What self-discipline! Maybe there was hope for me yet.

Connie pulled up in front of Kerrie's home but didn't park because there were no spaces.

"I know who Sadie is," I said, grabbing my tote bag from the back. I said it kind of cavalierly, like "Oh, and

153

you mean you haven't figured it out yet? What's taking you so long?"

Connie's mouth fell open. I am not making this up. At least I got a tiny crumb of my gratification-cake.

"You *what?*" she asked, incredulously. "Who *is* she? How'd you find out?"

"I'll explain later. But I know she's really Sarah McEvoy, Melinda McEvoy's daughter. And she's eighteen, not fifteen. Look, I've got to go." I pointed to the cars behind her that couldn't get down the narrow street until she moved.

"You better explain! I want to know how you found out." Then she smiled as she gripped the stick shift to push the car into gear. "Way to go, Bianca. I'm impressed."

Wow. Another little piece of my fantasy coming true. Connie telling me I impressed her. This was weird.

On that high, I walked up to Kerrie's house and gave the brass knocker a few sharp whacks.

Kerrie's house was tiny but pristine. The brick front had been stripped of its multi-colored formstone, and sand-blasted to an unnatural cleanliness. The door was painted a shiny gray-green, which Kerrie once told me was a special paint mixed after computers replicated a paint chip found on the original door dating back to 1810. The windows were new and secure, but they had been specially made to copy old paned windows, which were lovely, but hard to clean. Trust me, I know. I clean ours.

Kerrie came to the door in a few seconds, ushering me in with a kind of breathless excitement. I said hi to Mr. and Mrs. Daniels, Kerrie's mom and dad, who were reading in the living room, looking as if they were posing for a magazine spread on peaceful parenting.

We went first to the back of the house and the kitchen. There the smell of cider and pumpkin bread and other good fall things made me drool. While we had a quick snack, Kerrie went over her decorating schemes. Her mother briefly showed up to offer help, but Kerrie sweetly shooed her away.

Then, it was up to Kerrie's room for my hair treatment—a perfect time to share what I knew about Sadie with Kerrie and to discuss how to bring Sadie to whatever help she needed.

All in all, it promised to be a perfect afternoon—filled with exciting anticipation, juicy gossip, and social responsibility all at the same time.

Chapter Fifteen

Kerrie couldn't have had a better day for her party if she'd ordered it up special. The afternoon was bright and warm, but not so hot that the evening wouldn't be perfect.

Halloween time was an iffy weather proposition in the Baltimore area. Well do I remember the years when Mom had made me a nice warm costume, and then I'd been forced to sweat through trick-or-treating under layers of bunny fur. Then there were the years when I was garbed in thinner fabrics during unpredictable cold snaps—I remember a really pretty princess costume I had to cover up with a ratty parka because of the chilly night air. That still brings a tear to my eye.

Well, not really.

It wasn't Halloween night, of course, but I figured this gorgeous evening was kind of a compensation for all those Halloweens I'd suffered through because of Baltimore's fickle weather.

Kerrie decided to set my hair in pin curls, which we

did in her room shortly after I arrived. Her room was a teenager's dream. No fluffy pink pillows or bed sheets, no ruffled curtains and stuffed animals.

Well, okay, so she had a few teddy bears (none imported from China or third-world countries using slave labor). But the rest of the room was in red and gold, her bed set beneath a canopy of filmy fabrics purposely suggesting an Arabian nights theme. Her windows didn't even have curtains. Instead, she had dark maroon shades to keep out the light, and multi-colored beads strung above and around the window. She had her own TV and phone and computer, all set on pieces of furniture that looked like they'd been made just to house those items.

Although it was small, Kerrie's room felt comfortable. Everything had a place, and she kept everything in its place. Whenever I left Kerrie's room, I always had an irresistible urge to redecorate (and clean up) my own humble space.

While she fooled with my hair, I gave her the scoop on Sadie's identity.

Kerrie stood, slackly holding a hairbrush in one hand.

"What in the world is she still doing in school if she's eighteen? I mean she's in our class. She's a sophomore! Who in their right mind would want to repeat all that?" Kerrie asked, shrugging.

"Good question," I said, hoping the answer would come to me. I'd learned that sometimes just talking was a way to get at a question, so I thought I'd try that technique, and started babbling away. It worked in class sometimes when the teacher caught me off guard. Even moderately coherent rambling would eventually lead me to some sort of conclusion, usually with a few well-placed and helpful prods from the teacher. Maybe the same thing would happen here.

"She could be hiding," I said, "and high school is where she'd hide easiest."

"Bianca, if she's hiding, high school kind of locks her in. She'd be better off getting a job or something."

"She doesn't look like she needs a job," I said, offering more details of Sadie's living arrangements as far as I could make them out. "Unless, of course, she's living on borrowed time."

Kerrie sucked in her breath and pulled tightly on a strand of hair.

"Ouch."

"Well, that's creepy," Kerrie said. "You make it sound like she's got some incurable disease."

"No, I meant maybe she only has a certain amount of money and she needs to make more."

"Right. So why isn't she working?"

"Because she wants to finish her education? Isn't that what we're all told—stay in school and get a better job, or have a better career, or be all you can be?"

"That's the Army. But yeah, you have a point." Kerrie neatly twirled my hair into a perfect pin curl, securing it with a bobby pin. "Maybe she never finished high school."

"Hey! We could find out, couldn't we? Now that we know her name. If she's eighteen, she would have graduated from one of the schools in Salinas, right? And a lot of schools post their graduates' names, right? Maybe on their Web sites?"

"That would take a lot of digging." Kerrie pulled yet another strand and did the curling routine.

"That's what investigative work is all about, Kerrie. It's not all glamorous, Nancy Drew stuff."

"Nancy *who?*"

I said nothing, waiting for the moment she finished with my hair. When she did, she immediately logged onto a search engine and I stood in back of her, directing her through various web sites. Man, oh, man this was luxury. Unlimited time on the computer. No half-hour rules. No fear of the executioner's axe coming down on your neck. And a screaming fast line, too.

We managed to find a few schools, including the one from which Sadie ostensibly "transferred." No Sarah McEvoy was listed in the "We're proud of our graduates" pages.

"She's a drop-out," Kerrie said firmly. She turned around and looked at me with wide, serious eyes. "And she's getting her high school diploma by pretending to be younger than she is."

"This kind of jibes with something I've felt about Sadie for awhile." I sat on the edge of Kerrie's bed and grabbed one of her teddy bears to hold in my lap. "She always seems to me like she's starting over, like she's got a second chance at things and she doesn't want to blow it. I'm not exactly sure why."

"I'm in a bunch of classes with her," Kerrie said. "She always gets her work in on time, and it's good from what I've seen of it in oral presentations. And another thing—she actually gets stuff done early. If we have two weeks for an assignment, Sadie's done in a couple days. I've seen her hand in papers that have been typed and ready for weeks."

"Wow, Kerrie. Since when did *you* turn into Ace Snooper?"

Kerrie hit me good-naturedly with a feather by her desk. "I'm just observant, that's all. But I agree with you. I get the impression she wants to do really well, and not to please the teachers or parents or anything like that. She wants to do well for herself."

"She's coming tonight, right? You're sure?"

"As sure as I can be. Why?"

"I think we need to confront her. I can't think of one good reason why she'd be running this scam. I think she's in trouble. I think we should offer to help."

To my surprise, Kerrie didn't immediately agree. She cocked her head to one side and twisted her mouth as she thought about it. "What if we mess it all up for her?" she said at last. "I mean, what if she *is* starting over? Maybe we should let her finish her studies and get on with her life. If we confront her, we might scare her away."

"I have a feeling she's scared about something to begin with. And I think she might like a helping hand. We won't rat on her. Just encourage her to seek help. And maybe I'll think of a way to do it so that she won't be afraid we'll tattle. Okay?"

"Okay. It's a deal." Kerrie stood. "Come on, we have to start decorating."

By the time we were done, the house looked like it was ready to be featured on a Martha Stewart Halloween Special. Kerrie had thought of everything. She had twinkly orange and white lights strung up in the dining room, kitchen, and the small yard. She had a shrieking, movement-activated, spider hanging right outside the front door. She had candles and balloons and lights set in paper bags that were cut out with pumpkin designs.

And yes, she had pumpkins—scads of them, in all sizes, some cut into fantastic faces, some plain. And corn husks and stalks, and even a couple of bales of hay to sit on in the yard.

Her father helped us wire the stereo so it could be heard both inside and outside. Her mother helped mix up a special punch, and set out soda, cider, cups, and plates on a picnic table.

Our planning may have been fantastic, but we had so much fun decorating that we lost track of time. Only thirty minutes were left until zero hour and my hair was still in pin curls and Kerrie was still in jeans and T-shirt. Well, so was I, but the hair is the important thing.

Kerrie's mom shooed us upstairs while she finished with the food. There wasn't much left to do anyway. We were ordering in pizzas.

In a few breathless minutes, we were both shrieking and screaming as we donned our costumes and put on makeup. Kerrie's costume was as spectacular as mine. Layers of muted chiffon covered her legs, while a red beaded top with little cap sleeves edged in gold came to her midriff. She pulled her hair up in a bun and capped the whole thing off with a tiny hat adorned with veils that draped becomingly around her face.

"Now, on to you!" she said with a flourish, removing my pin curls as I sat in front of her vanity.

I was scared. Hair styling was serious business. When Kerrie pulled her brush through the mass of curls, I became even more scared than any scary movie could make me. All of a sudden, I felt like I'd made a big mistake. My hair was like a giant frizz ball, standing out a good three inches from my head in a white girl's Afro.

It was a veritable hair explosion, and I could swear there were casualties.

"Kerrie," I said softly, trying hard to hide my dismay. "Do something. Maybe flatten it with some water."

Kerrie was unruffled. With a deft pull on the brush (that nonetheless made me cry out in pain), she started smoothing my hair down. She grabbed a can of styling mousse and squirted on some foamy stuff, then brushed and brushed and brushed again until I thought she was trying to calm the frizz by brushing the hair out of my head. Literally. As in "pulling the hairs out with the brush." It certainly felt that way.

I couldn't look. I closed my eyes and let her do her best. If all else failed, I was going to run into the shower, smear the whole thing down with water, and then hide it all under the cloche hat. Skillful makeup would have to bring out my other features.

I thought maybe she had the same idea because after awhile I felt her pulling the tight little hat on my head and securing it with a few pins. The pain stopped. Kerrie was finished.

"Open up, Bianca. It's not that bad."

I held my breath, and cautiously opened my eyes.

Not that bad? Not that bad? It was gorgeous! I didn't recognize that girl in the mirror.

Gone was my "sorry, I didn't mean to give the impression I thought I was pretty" look, complete with mussed hair and pale features. In its place was someone sophisticated and suave, someone who combed her hair.

With her constant brushing, Kerrie had made my hair fall into neat shiny waves that bustled out from under the cloche hat in a charmingly soft cloud. With the make-up and the dress, I looked pretty. Not "maybe I am but I'll just pretend I'm not" pretty. Really pretty. Pretty as in "I know I look good and I don't care."

This was a whole new experience for me. I was going to start paying more attention to my hair and dress after this night.

"Well?" Kerrie put the hairbrush down on the vanity and stared at me in the mirror.

"Well, it's great! Thanks." I reached up and touched it to make sure it was real. "Do you think you could come over every day and do this before school?"

Kerrie laughed. "You come over here. And you set it every night."

"Hmm . . . I don't know about that." Staring in the mirror, I was beginning to think that pin-curls every night really wasn't all that steep a price to pay for this kind of loveliness.

"We better get moving." Kerrie picked up a fan to go with her costume and opened her bedroom door. "Want to get my CDs all lined up. And the candles lit."

Kerrie's mom and dad oohed and aahed over us when we went downstairs, but there wasn't much time for soaking up compliments. The CD organization alone occupied a great deal of thought and discussion. Then we had the candles to light, punch to put out, tables to arrange. Time passed quickly, which was a good thing because there's nothing worse than pre-party jitters. Well, some things are worse. But pre-party stomach flips are no fun either.

In fact, we were occupied with a major restructuring of the backyard party space when the first guests started to arrive. Kerrie decided, at the last minute, that her tiny backyard would probably end up as the most popular gathering spot. In order to make more room there, she wanted to move the family's gas grill into the basement and replace it with some more chairs. Her dad obliged after trying to talk her out of it, and she and her mom dusted off some old lawn chairs from the basement. The first guests helped us set them up against the high wooden fence that walled in the Daniels's patch of yard.

The music was pulsing away and folks were actually laughing when Doug arrived. True to his word, he was dressed as an FBI agent. Wearing a suit that looked a tad too big for him, he sported dark sunglasses, a phony laminated ID that would have fooled anybody in the dark yard, and a grim countenance that broke into a wide and fanciful grin when he saw me.

That's right. Doug really lit up when he saw me. He even said, "Bianca, you look fantastic!" It was as if the air had been knocked right out of me. Really.

I had trouble speaking. I didn't know what to say. I mumbled something like "Thanks." Or maybe it was "Tanks." Or "Yanks." My mouth wasn't working right. All I know was that my world started to swirl when he came over and grabbed my elbow and led me to one of those recently dusted lawn chairs, and then asked me if I wanted a soda or something.

"Yes. That would be great. There's going to be pizza," I managed to say.

Doug was back in a few minutes with a cola for me and a root beer for him and before you could say "trick-or-treat" we were actually talking and finally getting to know each other. It was great. I hadn't realized what a really cool guy he is. He wants to be an engineer, he told me. And maybe work for NASA or something like that.

"Have you thought about what you want to study in college?" he asked me.

"Um, law, or uh, justice, prosecuting . . . things," I said, "although I wouldn't mind doing what my sister does. Private investigating." I was just about to tell him about my sort-of investigation of Sadie when the pizzas arrived, and right after them came another crowd of partygoers.

To my surprise and Kerrie's delight, almost everyone wore costumes. There were presidential masks, French maids, apes, soldiers, and animals. There was even a ghost or two.

As Doug and I ate a piece of pizza a few minutes later, I noticed a thin, dark wraith standing alone, near the gate to the alley. It was Sadie. She *had* come.

Despite my growing closeness to Doug, I couldn't resist. I had to find out.

"Sarah," I called out just loud enough for her to hear. "Sarah McEvoy."

She turned and looked, her eyes wide with fear, her mouth slightly open.

Chapter Sixteen

A second later, Sadie turned and started toward the kitchen. She was going to leave! I couldn't let her. Not now. Not after coming so far, and getting so close.

"Doug, would you get me another soda? I want to say hi to Sadie." I jumped up and ran after Sadie while Doug dutifully went over to the refreshment table.

The party was really going well by this time, which meant it was crowded. Wall-to-wall people. Hard-to-get-through. Lots of "excuse me's" just to travel a few feet. By the time I'd pushed my way into the warm kitchen, I was sure Sadie would be long gone.

She wasn't. She had been hampered by the same throngs of teeming humanity that had stopped me. Caught between a vampire and a goddess, Sadie was desperately trying to make her way into the living room and out onto the street.

(Good grief. That was Brenda Watson in the goddess outfit. Only Brenda would come up with an idea like that. Not only did she look spectacular with her creamy skin showing off under the artfully draped—

and very thin—white fabric. She got to explain to everybody exactly which goddess she was, which meant she had looks and small talk all rolled into one tidy package. But I digress.)

Sadie sensed movement behind her and turned to see me coming after her.

"Wait!" I yelled over the thumping music, giggles, chatter, and Brenda Watson's lecture on goddesses in Greco-Roman history.

Her mouth opening again, a perplexed-looking Sadie didn't move. That was good. I managed to push my way past a giant spider, a Batman (boy, was that costume ever a mistake on scrawny Bobby Lagusta), and two Zorros. I gently touched Sadie's elbow and directed her back through the kitchen.

"Why were you leaving? The party's just getting started." We stood on the tiny porch that overlooked the tiny yard.

"I—I don't know. Tired, I guess." Her face was white as a sheet and not because she'd smeared make-up on it either. This was the real thing. This was scared white. "I thought I heard someone—what did you call me?" She looked right in my eyes and I suspected she wanted me to say "Sadie." So I did.

"Sadie. Sadie Sinclair," I lied. Then genius struck. "Sadie Mauvais Sinclair." I nearly whispered it, but she heard it all the same and whitened again. "You stole her name. The artist who lives in the part of California where you're from. Sadie Mauvais Sinclair." I spoke rapidly as inspiration took hold. "You took her name as your own."

"I did not steal her identity." Sadie pounded her left fist on the railing for emphasis. "I didn't. You can't accuse me of that. I didn't do it." Tears started to come to her eyes. Exactly what Pandora's box was I opening here? (For an explanation on "Pandora's Box," please consult Greek expert Brenda Watson.)

"You're Sarah. Sarah McEvoy," I said quietly, reaching out to touch her hand. I didn't want her to feel threatened. I wanted to help her. "There's nothing wrong with that. Are you ashamed of it or something? You shouldn't be. Everybody thinks their family is embarrassing . . ."

I was rambling. And if anyone was embarrassing, it was me with my phony-baloney "my door is always open, I want to help you" guidance-counselor chit-chat.

A tear drifted down Sadie's cheek and I felt about as low as a real spider. Making someone cry (other than a sibling) did not rank high on my "great experiences" list.

"You don't understand," she said. "You don't know." She shook her head back and forth.

"I want to know. I want to help." I touched her elbow again and started to steer her down into the yard, where the crowd was a little thinner. "Come on. We can sit down and talk."

To my surprise and relief, she went with me. We'd just settled in on the chairs in the corner when Doug appeared with my drink.

"Here you go. You want something, Sadie?" he asked, smiling at me. "You really look great in that costume, Bianca. Jesse thinks so, too."

An endorsement by a friend of your crush is like winning the lottery. This was good stuff—stuff I needed to cash in on pronto.

Too many things were happening at once. Where was Kerrie when I needed her? Actually, she was playing hostess, making sure food and drink and music were in plentiful supply.

"Sadie wants a soda, too. Thanks, Doug." I smiled up at him and actually felt good about smiling, knowing that I looked good in my flapper costume. I had a sudden sense of clothes-nostalgia. Why couldn't I live in a time when dressing up was no big deal?

As soon as Doug left, I scooted closer to Sadie, dropping my head down so she could hear me speaking quietly.

"So you're really Sarah. What kind of trouble are you in?"

"I'm not in trouble," she insisted, shaking her head again. "I got out of trouble. Why can't everyone leave me alone?" Tears were welling up again, so I started talking fast.

"You're starting over. That's a great thing. Nobody can fault you for that. But what about Lemming Lady and Ice Man? Why are they after you?"

She looked at my like I was crazy. Uh-oh. Did I just say "Lemming Lady and Ice Man?" I really said that? Could someone please rewind the tape?

"I mean that woman and that man? Why are they after you?"

"They're not after me. They went away." Her voice took on an urgent, almost angry tone. "They needed to borrow some money. That's all. They were friends of my mother."

"Your mother died last year. I bet that was tough."

"Not so tough. Not as tough as other things." Sadie sounded as if she didn't mean it. In fact, her voice cracked a little when she spoke. "I can take care of myself. I have for a long time."

"How did your mother die? Was it an accident or something?"

Sadie stood abruptly. "I had nothing to do with it. Nothing. Leave me alone. You're not helping me, Bianca. Now that you know—I'll have to—you've ruined everything!" She stomped away just as Doug arrived on the scene with her drink.

"Hey, I thought she was thirsty!" He put the drink on a nearby table. The music stopped its *thwump-thwump* beat and turned into something mellow and slow. Doug looked over at me with a gaze that I can only describe as hungry. It sent a little shiver down my back.

Too bad nobody was dancing. If they were, he'd have asked me to dance. I'm sure of it. Instead, he reached over—and here things kind of slowed down as if the tape were being run at the wrong speed—and he grabbed—my—hand! Ay-chihuahua! Mama mia! Praise the Lord and pass the ammunition!

"Uh . . . well . . . I . . ." I said. Oh yeah. Great conversation. Way to go, Bianca. Remind me never to enter the Miss America contest. I'd fall to pieces on the questions part.

Doug didn't seem to mind. He maneuvered us back to the seats and settled in really close to me, his leg pressing up against mine. I swallowed. He smiled. It was dark in our little corner. His face came a little closer. I could smell Irish Spring soap on his cheek. His lids lowered. He was zeroing in for a kiss.

Sensory overload! I canna hold her any longer, Cap'n! Warning, warning!

His lips were just a millimeter away, which I knew because I was now trying to memorize every nanosecond of the experience, taking down each observation in some mental journal that I would reveal to Kerrie later that night.

But my powers of observation were my undoing. Just as he was about to plant his puckered mouth on mine, I caught movement out of the corner of my eye, through the slats in the tall wooden fence.

Lemming Lady! I knew her from the clack of her high-heeled boots as much as by her black outfit. And behind her, Ice Man.

Doug only had time to brush my lips with a gentle kiss before I pulled away. Sadie was at the gate, getting ready to leave. Despite what she had said about the Daring Duo, I knew they still wanted something from her, or had her in some kind of bind. They were trouble. And she was heading right into it. I shot up, surprising both Doug and myself.

"Sadie!" I called. Looking down at Doug, my heart screamed at my mind. "Idiot alert! You just left the Love of Your Life's first kiss because of Lemming Lady, Ice Man, and Sadie-Sarah? Are you *nuts?*"

"Doug," I said gently, "I think Sadie might need our help. Sorry." I pushed my way through the crowd as Sadie opened the gate. Even from a few feet away, I could see her reaction as she ran into Lemming Lady. Sadie's face was now ashen. They pushed their way into the party, backing her into the crowd. They fit right in. They looked like villains.

"Who are those two?" Doug asked, holding my arm. Thank goodness he hadn't given up on me.

"I don't know," I lied. "All I know is that they keep

bothering Sadie. Come on, let's go." Unfortunately, my progress was impeded by Nicole, who chose that moment to come up and gush about my costume. She was dressed as Little Orphan Annie and looked ready to burst into "Tomorrow." I tried to politely wrap up the mutual gushing and move on, but she was insistent, and was soon joined by another friend. Meanwhile, Sadie was angrily shaking her head, engaged in some heated conversation with the two just-arrived villains.

Doug came to the rescue! He walked on without me, striding to Sadie with a purposeful gait. He looked just like the FBI agent he was pretending to be—calm, menacing, and protective.

He looked so convincing, in fact, that Lemming Lady and Ice Man backed off before he even reached them. Before they slunk out into the alley, I saw Lemming Lady spit out some parting words to Sadie. Whatever she said, it acted like a bullet piercing Sadie's heart. She stepped back as if hit, then lunged back through the crowd toward the kitchen again.

Doug returned in a few seconds.

"What did she say?" I asked after escaping the clutches of Nicole and crew.

"Sadie? She didn't say anything."

"No. The other woman."

"I didn't catch all of it," Doug said. "It sounded like 'You killed your mother.' That's odd, don't you think? Is Sadie's mom mad at her or something?"

"No, no," I said. "Sadie's mom is dead."

Chapter Seventeen

There was no time for more elaborate explanations. And, sadly, no time for soft embraces in the autumn twilight. Sigh. That would have to wait for another night. Luckily for me, Doug seemed to be entranced by the new Bianca he was seeing. Not only was I beautiful tonight. I was interesting. I was onto something.

"Should we go after her?" he asked, looking at me eagerly.

I looked up. She was already at the kitchen door, trying to push her way through. My guess was she was heading to her car, to escape. I made a snap decision.

"I'll go after her and talk to her. You find Kerrie. Tell her Sadie might be in trouble and is leaving, and that I'm going to try to talk her out of it."

He grinned at me and looked like he might punch me in the arm, the same kind of good-natured punch he'd landed on my shoulder in the mall so many moons ago (or at least it seemed that long ago). Rats, I wanted more than a punch in the shoulder. Hadn't we just progressed beyond that hail-fellow-well-met stage? His thoughts exactly. He put his arm around my shoulders and gave me a warm squeeze that communicated fondness, good cheer, admiration, respect, honor . . . well, maybe not all those things. But a couple of them at least.

"Okay, Bianca. Where should we catch up with you?"

"Uh. Out front." Sadie was inside. I had to hurry. "Somewhere out front." I sped off, pushing through the crowd so forcefully they probably thought I was ill and needed the bathroom fast. Whatever. It did the trick. The costumed aliens, freaks, ghosts, and fairy tale figures parted like the Red Sea before Charleton Heston.

In the kitchen, I saw Sadie's black-robed, wraith-like figure disappear beyond the doorway to the dining room.

"Excuse me," I said to a masked Barbie doll. (Barbie doll? Who would wear a Barbie doll costume? I didn't want to know.) "Excuse me!" I accidentally stepped on Barbie's toe. Really. She shrieked. But she moved aside nonetheless. Soon I was at the doorway, but Sadie had gone through the dining room into the living room, where Mrs. Daniels was asking her if she needed a ride home.

"No, thanks, Mrs. Daniels. It was a great party. Tell Kerrie I said thanks."

"Is someone picking you up?" Kerrie's mom asked. She looked a little concerned. As much as they liked living in Fells Point, I don't think she was too keen on any of us kids walking around by ourselves. "Why don't you wait inside?"

"That's okay. She's with me," I said, arriving on the

scene like a superhero. Wonder Flapper. Action figure sales were sure to be in the billions. "Uh. Connie's coming for her. And, and I'll show Connie where she lives."

My improvisation wasn't enough to allay Mrs. Daniels's fears. She looked skeptical. "If she's not right out front," I added, "we'll come back in and wait." That did the trick, coming as it did with her husband's call for help in the kitchen.

Mrs. Daniels was barely gone a second when Sadie gave me the evil eye and pulled open the door so fast it nearly hit the wall. In a flash, she was outside, barely giving me time to figure out what was up, let alone go after her.

But go after her I did. She was running down the street and I was doing my best to keep up in my matching mauve-colored flapper shoes with tissue stuffed in the toes so they'd fit. If a "runs like a girl" contest had been held that night, I'd be champ.

It didn't take long to figure out where Sadie was headed. Her car was parked at the end of the block and she was pulling what looked like car keys from her jeans pocket under her black robe.

I wouldn't catch up in time. I needed something else to stop her.

"Sarah! Sarah McEvoy!" I shouted it so loud it echoed off the formstone and brick fronts of the row homes on the block. And it made Sadie stop in her tracks and turn around.

"Stop that. Please," she hissed at me, before continuing on her way.

Hobbling forward as fast I could, I tried another message from the past.

"Sarah! Talk to me. Come on, Sarah." Inspiration. "I know you didn't kill your mother."

The same bolt that had hit her when Lemming Lady had thrown the accusation her way in Kerrie's small yard now stopped her again. She stood super still. Her back to me, she leaned her head forward, looking as if she was breathing hard, like she was throwing up or something.

When I caught up with her, I found she wasn't sick to her stomach. She was sick at heart. Big gulping sobs were convulsing her body. She pulled her fist to her mouth as if to cork it, but it didn't do the trick.

Remember what I said about feeling lower than a spider when I'd made her eyes water before? Well, you could have scraped me off the bottom of a shoe, that's how low I felt now. At least I'd stopped her, though. At least I could talk to her.

"Sarah," I said. Gently putting my arm on her shoulder, I tried to look into her eyes. "Sarah, you have to tell me what's wrong. Why are those people trying to frame you? What are you running away from?" I wanted to lead her back to the house, but she resisted.

"In the car," she said between gasping tears. She unlocked the passenger side and I slid in while she walked around to the driver's seat.

I started talking as soon as she was inside. "I know people who could help you. My sister's a private investigator. Kerrie's father is . . ."

"I tried calling your sister," Sadie volunteered.

"I know."

"But it was hard to explain." She sniffled. I wished I had some tissues. Hey, I did have some! Part of my

176

costume was a thin change-purse on a long gold chain. Kerrie had put tissues and breath spray in it for me when we were changing. I made a mental note to praise Kerrie for her planning skills.

"Here." I offered Sadie a tissue and she gratefully accepted, blowing her nose and wiping her eyes. "So, what can we do? Do you want me to get Connie on the case again? Why are they trying to frame you for murder? And who are they? Why do you give them money?" Yes, indeed, I was taking the slow and subtle approach. Luckily for me, Sadie was confused enough not to notice my less-than-spectacular interviewing skills. As she calmed down, she started to talk.

"My mother died in an accident. I was driving."

You could have punched me in the gut and not gotten a stronger reaction. I knew kids with family problems. I knew kids with their own problems. I knew kids who walked too close to the sad side of empty. But I never knew anyone who felt responsible for the death of a parent. Death of a parent was bad enough. When that parent died in a car accident and you were driving? I trembled at the thought. Too much guilt and too much pain for someone Sadie's age.

"I'm sorry," I murmured. "Do you need money? Do you need a place to stay?"

"No," Sadie said, sniffling again. "I've got money. From her life insurance."

Realization dawned. "That's how you afford your condo!" I said. I felt like knocking my head with the flat of my hand. Of course.

"Sort of. It belonged to—to someone I knew. I'm just 'borrowing' it."

Uh-oh. Didn't sound good. Everybody knows that "borrowing" is a euphemism for "stealing." I went back to my original tactic—offering help.

"Well, if you can't 'borrow' it any more, I'm sure we can find a place for you to stay. Why don't you tell me about why you contacted Connie? I help her with her cases a lot, you know."

That was a little half-truth, which is really a euphemism for "lying." It didn't make me feel good, but I was too charged up to think about it at the moment. I put that on my to-do list for another day. Ponder the moral consequences of telling half-truths in order to help someone in trouble.

"Oh no!" Sadie sat up straight and looked in her rearview mirror.

"What?"

"They're back there. They'll see me. They'll come after me. They'll come after you! I have to get out of here!"

Without giving me a glance, she turned the ignition and gunned the engine. In a few seconds, she was screeching out of the parking spot while I struggled to put on my seat belt.

"Who are they anyway, Sadie?" I turned around and saw Lemming Lady and Ice Man's big black car. My mind did a flash back to the fear I'd felt when they followed my bus. These were not pleasant people. No Mister and Miss Congeniality prizes for them. "Maybe we should call the police."

"No!" Sadie's sadness had given way to anger. She sped down the narrow streets with grim determination, muttering a curse under her breath as she continually checked the rear- and side-view mirrors.

"What do they want, Sadie?" I grabbed the dashboard to steady myself as she flew around a corner.

"Damn it!" she cried out. "I'm almost out of gas!"

I turned around. They were closing fast. There was no way Sadie was going to lose that pair. They had more power, and probably more gas. I looked at her. She was chewing her lower lip, and her brows came together in a worried "v." "Sadie," I insisted. "Let's call the police."

She didn't respond. Instead, she pulled the car over to the curb, gently gliding it into a spot with just a foot of the car on the legal side of "No Parking Beyond this Sign."

"Get down." She looked at me with wide eyes.

"What?"

"Scoot down in the car. They probably didn't see you."

"What are you going to do?" I took off my seat belt and did as she said, scrunching into the space under the dashboard in front of my seat.

"I'm going to go with them. That's what they want. It'll be bad news if they think you're involved in this, trying to help me."

Before I could protest, she opened the door, stepped out, and slammed the door shut. I heard another car slow down and muffled voices talking. Then, I heard Sadie's voice loud and clear.

"All right. All right. I'll do it again. Just get off my case. And leave my friends alone."

Chapter Eighteen

As soon as I heard the car zoom away, I was on the sidewalk, getting oriented. Fells Point isn't my normal hang-out and Sadie had managed to drive us a few blocks down and over. Mentally retracing the route, I started back toward Kerrie's house.

I ran as fast as I could for one block, looked down at those wonderful shoes that made my feet look so slender and chic, and stopped to take the shoes off. Now I could gather more speed, even if the dress did keep me from taking long strides. The rough pavement chewed up my light stockings, though, so by the time I arrived at Kerrie's block, my flapper look now included interesting vertical stripes up my legs caused by runs in my hose.

Not even bothering to knock, I ran into the Daniels's house, searching for Kerrie and Doug. I found them in the dining room, huddled near the kitchen door. When she saw me, Kerrie screeched as if seeing a ghost.

"Bianca, I was so worried about you. Doug and I

didn't know what to do. I was going to tell my parents!" Kerrie said.

I pulled Kerrie and Doug away from the crowds into the quiet dining room, and explained what I knew about Sadie.

"Well, we should tell the police. Or my dad," Kerrie said.

"I don't know." I put my shoes on the floor and stepped into them again. Ouch. After flat-footing it for five blocks, my toes were a little cramped. "She's done something that keeps her from going to the police. That's my bet."

Doug stepped up next to me. "Like what?"

"I don't know." I leaned on the table a little. I was beat. The adrenaline rush from my encounter with Doug and then with Sadie was beginning to wear off. I had to sit down. As if reading my mind, Doug pulled out a chair for me.

"Whatever it is, it's got to be something she does, or has done, for that man and woman," I said. I slumped into the chair and held my head in my hands. Kerrie and Doug pulled out chairs, too, with Doug sitting right next to me. It was crystal clear to me by now that Doug was beginning to think of us as a couple. I felt tingly all the way down to my pinched toes.

"Just the facts. That's what Connie says. Review the facts." I was thinking out loud. "Sadie is being threatened by that man and woman. My guess is they're threatening to frame her for her mother's death. The reason they're doing it is because they want something from her."

"Money?" Doug asked.

"She's given them money in the past," I explained,

telling him about the incident at the ATM machine. And then, since the moment was right, I added the part about how I'd missed our first date at the movies because I'd been trying to help Sadie. Okay, so I had been following her more than helping her. But I always *meant* to help her.

Doug was appropriately impressed. "Gee, Bianca, you should have told me that's why you stood me up. I would have understood."

We stared moon-eyed at each other for a few seconds until Kerrie broke in with a dose of reality. "Whatever they want, she's obviously agreed to give it to them. If we want to help her, we better do it now. I don't think we'll see much of her after tonight, do you?"

"No," I said, "you're right. We won't." I stood up. If we didn't help Sadie tonight, we wouldn't be able to help her at all. She'd be gone. I was certain of it.

Doug stood, too. "I can drive. Where do you want to go?"

Both Kerrie and I looked at him, our heads moving together in one smooth synchronous motion to face him.

"You can drive?" I sputtered.

"Just got my license today." He reached into his pocket and proudly pulled out and displayed a laminated card with a mug shot that made him look like he'd been caught doing something wrong. "Didn't want anyone to know I was taking the test," he added sheepishly.

I looked at Doug with new, admiring eyes. He'd passed his driver's test. This was a man.

"Okay. Let's go." I took charge. "Sadie's house. She'll take them back there and pick up her stuff."

Kerrie backed off. "I don't like this at all. Bianca, I have to tell my dad." Her eyes glistened with tears.

And she was right. This was serious business. But I wasn't ready just yet to throw in the towel and call up the reserves. Maybe, just maybe, if I could get to Sadie and get her to finish telling me her story before any police were involved, things would be better for her.

"All right," I agreed. "But let me talk to Sadie first. That's all I'm asking. Then we'll talk to your father, okay?"

Kerrie didn't look happy, but finally she nodded her assent. "If I don't hear from you in an hour, I'm telling my dad."

"I don't have a phone," I said.

"Wait a minute. I'll lend you my cell phone. You can call me and let me know when you find her!" She ran upstairs and was down a few seconds later, the phone in one hand and a slip of torn paper in the other.

"Here." She handed me the phone, then the paper. "I think this is Sadie's phone number. From that criss-cross directory."

Again, I felt like slapping my head with my hand. Kerrie had had Sadie's number all along, ever since I'd told her Sadie's address, the night Connie and I had found Sadie in the Barrington Arms. Kerrie must have looked it up in her father's "backwards" directory—matching it to the condo's address.

Doug and I quickly made our way back to the street. Once there, he put his arm around my shoulder. This was great. This was neat. This was obviously something he'd given some thought to. He'd planned to use this party as the device to ratchet up our relationship.

I was impressed. He drove. He planned. He wanted to help find Sadie. How much luckier could a girl get?

Well, there *was* one thing. Once in his parents' little Honda, it became painfully clear that Doug was still a novice at this driving thing.

"I don't drive in the city much," he explained as we immediately headed in the wrong direction. Somehow, Doug managed to get us on St. Paul Street going south. We needed to go north. You would think that the harbor being in the way would have been a dead giveaway that we were not on the right track. When he starting humming cheerfully to himself as he headed around Federal Hill on the other side of the harbor, I pointed out his mistake.

"Uh, Doug, I think you need to go up Charles Street. North. Towson's north." He took this friendly tip in stride, but by the time he had us turned around, we'd lost precious minutes. Or maybe it was precious hours at the rate he was going.

Unlike a lot of guys who like to show off by getting up some velocity, Doug seemed quite content to mosey along at the speed limit, even a hair under it. Any other time, I might have found this endearing. But tonight I felt like reaching over with my foot and squashing his down on the accelerator pedal until the tires squealed.

"We better hurry," I said after clearing my throat. "She's probably already there."

"Why don't you call her?" he asked as he slowed down for a green light.

"Call her?" Oh yes. The cell phone. I whipped it out and punched in her number from the paper Kerrie had given me. It rang and rang and rang. Darn it. Maybe she'd already left. Maybe she hadn't even gone there. Maybe she hadn't gotten there yet.

I tried another number. Home. Voice mail picked up. Hey, who was on the phone? What about the half hour rule? (I was sure whoever was on the phone had already been on for twenty-five minutes. Or maybe even twenty-eight.)

I clicked off and held the phone in my lap as we meandered up Charles Street. At this rate, I figured we'd be at Sadie's condo in a day or two.

"No luck, huh?" Doug asked. When he turned to look at me, he turned the steering wheel a bit too far and a guy in the lane next to us beeped the horn. And said a few things. Loudly. And unpleasantly. Doug concentrated on the road.

"No luck." I picked up the phone and hit the redial button. Voice mail again. Now I was steaming. Nobody has to obey the half hour rule but me? Was there some sort of hidden message encoded in my mother's instructions? Something like—everyone else can have free use of the phone except Bianca, who can only use it for a half hour at a time? I must have missed that part.

I'd try Connie's cell phone. Clicking off again, I quickly dialed her number. It rang and rang and rang and then kicked over to voice mail, too.

After that frustrating experience, I figured all that

was left to do was sit back and enjoy our leisurely ride. I'd try Sadie again in a few minutes.

But in a few seconds, my phone starting ringing. Or rather, playing "The Toreador Song." At first I thought it was a radio from a nearby car. Then Doug pointed to the phone in my lap (and veered a little to the right while he did it). "You better get that," he said while he ignored the shouts of the driver next to us.

"Hello," I said tentatively.

"Hello," a female voice said in reply. "Who is this?"

"Who is *this?*" I asked haughtily. After all, this girl was calling me. I wasn't calling her.

"You just called my cell phone," she said. "Who is this? Why'd you call me? Is this Trina?"

The voice sounded familiar. "Connie?" I asked.

"Bianca?"

"How'd you get this number?" I asked.

"Caller ID on my phone."

"Why didn't you answer when I phoned? Where are you?"

"Out."

"You're on a date!" I nearly screamed. Connie was on a hot date and hadn't wanted to be interrupted. Come to think of it, she sounded a little breathless. "With Kurt!"

"What of it? Now, why'd you call me?"

"I'm trying to find Sadie." I explained everything. Well, not exactly everything. Not the parts about Sadie saying to leave her friends alone, or the part where Sadie might be on the wrong side of the law. "Where are you?" I asked.

"Uh. Over in Randallstown."

"Randallstown? What are you doing there?" I

asked. Randallstown was on the west side of the city. We didn't know anyone who lived in Randallstown. Hmm . . . Kurt! Maybe that's where he lived. But Randallstown was farther from Towson than we were.

No matter. The way Doug was driving, we'd be lucky to arrive at Sadie's in time for her twenty-first birthday party. Or maybe the birth of her first child.

"Can you head to Sadie's?" I asked. "You'll probably get there before us."

"Why? Where are you?" She sounded a little annoyed. Her date must have been going well.

"Stuck in traffic," I said.

"Hey, it's not too bad," Doug protested, letting the car drift to the left as he gestured in that direction. Luckily, no one was in that lane.

"Are you even sure that's where she is?" said Connie, sounding exasperated. I heard Kurt's voice in the background saying something that sounded like "What a mess." At least that's what I think he said. Otherwise, it could have been "I'll get dressed."

"I'll check. I'm going to call her. Give me a minute. I'll call you back." We hung up and I immediately redialed Sadie's number. To my shock, she actually picked up the phone on the sixth ring, just as I was about to give up. Her voice was low and tired. As soon as she said "hello," I plunged in talking.

"Sadie, it's me, Bianca. Doug and I are on our way over to your place. Don't say anything. Don't tell us not to come. Don't go away. We want to help you. We want to get you out of this mess. Uh, Kerrie's dad is a lawyer and he's agreed to help. You haven't done anything wrong. You can cut a deal."

Man, I was good. I was making stuff up right and

left. We hadn't talked to Kerrie's dad. And I had no idea exactly what kind of trouble Sadie was in. But my guess is that if she was nice enough to go off with Lemming Lady and Ice Man in order to protect her friends, she was worth helping.

She didn't say anything right away, which told me I'd hit a nerve. She was considering it. Then I heard Lemming Lady's voice in the background urging her to hurry and asking who it was.

"Nobody, Angelica. Just a telephone solicitor. Don't rush me. I'm beat. Plus I need to pack up my computer." Then she clicked off.

"Well?" Doug asked. He was getting better. This time when he looked at me he didn't bring the car with him. We were now near the outskirts of town and traffic was lighter.

"I think Sadie's going to wait for us. The woman who's after her is named Angelica. Let me tell Connie." I dialed my sister's cell phone and gave her the info. Then I asked her about Angelica and who she thought she was.

"Angelica what?" she asked. "What's her last name?" From the sound of it, I could tell that Connie and Kurt were getting in the car and heading off to Sadie's.

"I don't know. That's all she said—Angelica."

I heard Kurt's voice in the background. Then Connie spoke to him, not to me. She came back on the phone. "Look, Kurt says you shouldn't do anything once you get there. Just hang out in the parking lot until we show up. Keep an eye on the doors. Kurt used to be a bounty hunter, Bianca. He knows this stuff."

Wow! Connie was dating a former bounty hunter. And all I had was Doug the Diligent Driver. Hey, I wasn't complaining. Doug was all right by me.

We were now on the edge of Towson, just heading into the south side of the shopping and business district. Doug easily navigated this area. It was his home turf. I told him to go to the Barrington Arms and he was swiftly maneuvering through little side streets and onto main drags, clearly comfortable with where he was. His driving was better, too—more confident and less quirky. I explained to Connie that we were almost there.

We were in the parking lot by now and I saw the black vehicle that Angelica and her friend used.

"Their car is here. Angelica's and the guy's."

"Well, just stay out of sight. Give me a call if they leave."

Doug pulled into a spot down the row of cars from the black car, and cut the engine. He rolled his window down a crack and looked over at me with half closed eyes.

"Since we have to wait, why don't you scoot on over here?" he asked. "To keep warm?"

To keep warm? Need I tell you that I already was a bit warm? My face felt as if I'd been standing in front of a raging fire. My hands were just as toasty. In fact, I was so warm from an inner glow that I was sure I was tanning from the inside out.

Doing as Doug suggested, I unbuckled my seat belt and slid closer. In a second, he had his arm around me and was bending forward to give me that kiss that had been interrupted at Kerrie's party.

Sparks flew, fireworks went off, sirens wailed, the

world spun. All that and more. This was dangerous stuff. Doug was entrancing me and, much as I liked being entranced, I also liked being in control. Just as I pondered this new state of affairs, I heard the familiar click-clack of Angelica's two-inch platform heel boots on the hard asphalt.

Chapter Nineteen

Doug heard it, too. He straightened and pulled his arm away, looking out the back window of the car. Unfortunately, Doug had pulled the car into the spot rather than backing it in, so we had to twist and crane our heads to get a good look at what was happening. I don't think Doug was too good at back-ups.

"Let me call Connie," I whispered. I got her on the phone in a flash, and she told me that she and Kurt, though just a few blocks away, were having a hard time getting over to the Barrington Arms through a maze of unfamiliar streets. So Doug had one up on the hulky Kurt. Doug knew Towson. My Doug. My hero.

"They're getting in the car!" Doug hissed at me. He unlocked his door and started to get out.

"Doug!" I hissed back. "Don't let them see you."

Either he didn't hear me or he didn't listen because Doug slammed the door, not hiding his presence from the diabolical duo and Sadie. Except the diabolical duo was the Diabolical Uno. Only Angelica was walking toward the black car, hauling a big box with Sadie behind her carrying another box. Her computer.

"Bianca! Bianca! What's happening?" Connie's voice squawked at me from the cell phone.

"Doug got out of the car. I have to go after him," I whispered. I slid over to the door and unlocked it, then quietly left the car, being careful not to slam the door. Unlike Doug, I stayed down and out of sight. I had no idea what he was planning, but I wasn't comfortable with overt actions.

"Hey, you there! Hold it! What's in those boxes?" Doug said forcefully.

Doug was shouting at Sadie and Angelica in a strong voice. It was deeper than usual and sounded as if it came from someone in authority.

Come to think of it, it *was* The Voice of Authority, or what such a voice sounded like. Peering from my hiding space behind the right back fender of Doug's Honda, I could see that Doug had put on his sunglasses and was striding purposefully towards Sadie and Angelica. He was pretending to be an officer of the law, just what Angelica had thought he was when she'd seen him at the party! Doug had brains. Doug was cool. Doug was my guy.

Sadie played along.

"Angelica," she said. "You better do as he says." And then Sadie just dropped her box, smack in the middle of the parking lot. In fact, it sounded as if she threw it rather than dropped it.

Angelica was undaunted. She just sped up her pace, threw her box in the back seat of the black car, and yelled at Sadie to "come on!"

Uh-oh. I wasn't sure Doug had a counter punch to

Angelica's disregard for the law. Or the law that he was pretending to be. I crept forward, expecting to see Doug back off and come back to the car. Boy was I surprised.

Doug stopped in his tracks, spread his legs wide, and reached into his breast pocket, from whence he pulled out a—gun!

Yikes! A gun? Was he nuts? Was he certifiable?

"Halt! FBI!" he yelled at them. With both hands he aimed the shiny gun at Angelica. That stopped her. Open-mouthed, she stared at Doug, her hand resting on the edge of the car door. Sadie backed away from the car, equally surprised at the turn of events.

"Back away from the car," Doug said menacingly, a steely edge in his voice. He waved the gun ever so slightly to the left, indicating he wanted them to step out into the open part of the parking lot, away from the car. He was really getting into this. He was going for an Oscar with this performance.

Only trouble was, what was the denouement? What was he planning on doing with Angelica and Sadie once he had them? He couldn't possibly have handcuffs, too. And what would we do—make a citizen's arrest for violating nice-person rules?

As Doug moved towards them, I caught Angelica looking back at the condo. My gaze followed hers and zeroed in on what she saw. Ice Man! He was headed their way, silently coming up on Doug from behind. And he was reaching into his jacket, too. My heart went on a roller coaster ride. My ears rang. My mind screamed. I had to do something or Ice Man would do something that I didn't even want to think about.

Where were Connie and Kurt? Come on! If Doug could find his way through Towson, surely bounty hunter Kurt could. He'd been this way before, too.

Sweat covered my brow even though it was cool outside. Doug was to my left. Ice Man was to my right. If I stepped out and screamed, would Ice Man do something desperate—like aim his gun at Doug or me? Would Doug turn around and shoot? Ay-yay-yay. We hadn't covered these problems in our "Religious and Moral Dilemmas in the New Millennium" class. And somehow I suspected that Sister Rose Marie Cornish didn't have this situation anywhere in the syllabus.

I nervously placed my strand of beads in my mouth. The beads! The beads would slow Ice Man down. I ripped the strands over my head and chewed furiously on the string that held them together while I sneaked up toward Ice Man, cowering below the car lines. He was walking slowly toward Doug, so I would soon be within bead-shooting range.

Crazy things go through your head at times like these. I started wondering how to calculate exactly when my progress forward would meet up with Ice Man's progress toward Doug. It was like a math problem—a criminal traveling at five miles an hour leaves his end of the parking lot at 10:05, while a flapper traveling at three miles an hour leaves her end of the parking lot at 10:06. When will the two meet?

I vowed to pay more attention in Honors Algebra.

There was no time for math regrets now. I figured if I could get close to Ice Man, I could start spraying him with beads, and maybe he'd think they were bugs or something. I'd throw them at him until he stopped.

Or until Connie arrived. Where *was* Connie anyway, I thought for the millionth time.

Ba-boom, ba-boom, my heart was saying. I gulped. I positioned the beads in my fingers, ready to draw them off one-by-one and pummel Ice Man.

Ah, the best-laid plans often end up as guacamole in the blender of life. Just as I was about to start my bead-shooting routine, something happened. I dropped the strands. All of them at once. Like glassy rain, they bounced and pinged on the asphalt, gliding across the parking lot in a hundred thousand shards of gleaming glass.

"What the—?" Ice Man said, looking down. It was too late. He'd stepped forward into the sparkling mess before realizing what was happening. Like it or not, Ice Man was now Skating Man, the beads acting like ball bearings under his feet.

He wasn't very good at skating, either. He had no grace, no panache. No balance. In a few seconds, the ground had been swept from under him and he was on his back, the gun flying from his hand into the air, where it was caught by . . .

Kurt! Kurt and Connie chose that moment to squeal into the parking lot, coming up behind Ice Man just in time for Kurt to reach out the driver's window and pluck the gun from the air. Did someone choreograph this thing or what?

Connie and Kurt exited the Jeep and came around to help. I stood up and let my presence be known.

Angelica glared at me and sneered, "You!" Which I took as a compliment.

Kurt took care of Ice Man while Connie grabbed Angelica and told Doug to put his "piece" away.

With a broad smile, Doug stuck the end of his gun in his mouth.

And began to chew it.

"Gummy candy," he said. "I thought it looked pretty cool."

I ran forward to hug him, not caring if Connie saw me draped over my boyfriend. She smiled.

And so did Sadie.

It took a couple of hours to get everything straightened out. Doug and I took Sadie back to Kerrie's house while Connie and Kurt handled Angelica and Dwayne. Yup, that's what Ice Man's name is—Dwayne Norton.

At Kerrie's, the party was still rolling, although the crowd had considerably thinned out, so we were able to seclude ourselves in Mr. Daniels's study on the second floor while Sadie told us the whole story and Mr. Daniels gave her advice.

Most of it was stuff I'd already figured out, which made me feel really smart. I wished I could get them all to sign affidavits attesting to my brilliance so I could wave it under Connie's nose in the future.

Sadie was Sarah McEvoy and, as I had surmised, she was an eighteen-year-old high school dropout. Her mother had hung with some bad folks, so Sadie's life hadn't been too pleasant. After Sadie dropped out of high school, she worked in a computer store, which is where she'd met Angelica, who worked there, too.

In their spare time, Sadie would show Angelica all sorts of things you could do on the computer. Sadie was a whiz at it. When Angelica got sacked, Sadie was friendless. But not for long. Angelica came back asking Sadie for help. She told her she had a cousin who was in trouble.

"She gave me the woman's name, social security number, and birth date and asked me if I could access her credit card on the computer because Angelica said she wanted to pay her bill for her. I did it. I didn't know what she was really doing." Sadie sniffled and leaned forward in the straight-back chair next to Mr. Daniels' desk. Doug and I stood near the door and Kerrie sat on the edge of the desk.

"What was she doing?" Mr. Daniels asked patiently. He handed Sadie a tissue.

"She—and Dwayne—were stealing people's identities. She wanted access to the credit cards so she could use them. I didn't know."

"So you worked for them?" Mr. Daniels asked.

"Yes. For nearly a year. I was stupid. I thought Angelica was my friend. She'd give me little bits of information about people she said were her friends or relatives, then ask me to access their bank records, their credit card records. Then she asked me to open a corporate checking account for Dwayne, which I did. And then I figured out what was going on." Sadie held the tissue in her hands between her legs. "Will I go to jail?" she asked pitifully.

"I don't think so," Kerrie's dad said. "I think we can avoid that. How did you figure out what was going on?"

"One of the so-called relatives Angelica was supposedly helping had been a customer. That's probably where she got the person's address and credit card number to begin with—from receipts or checks. Anyway, this person came in the store again to buy something. Her credit card showed she was maxed out, and she was flabbergasted. She said she hardly used her credit card. She couldn't understand it. After she left the store, I remembered Angelica asking me to access her records a couple months earlier. I checked them out again and found out Angelica had not paid off her debt or helped her. In fact, a whole long list of purchases had been racked up since Angelica had asked me to hack into her account. That's when I figured it out."

"And what did you do?"

"I told Dwayne and Angelica I couldn't help them anymore."

"And?"

"And they went away for awhile. But then my mother died." Sadie started to cry in earnest as she told the story of her mother's death. The car Sadie had been driving—her mother's boyfriend's vehicle—was rammed when someone ran a stoplight. Sadie's mother hadn't been wearing a seat belt.

Sadie wiped her eyes with the tissue. "I got a lot of insurance money I didn't know she had. Dwayne came by one night and told me he could make the police believe I had killed her, that I had caused the accident deliberately. He said he was going to frame me for murder and nobody would believe me because I was already guilty of identity-theft and I had a record. At the very least, the cops would get me on the identity fraud rap."

"A record?" Kerrie's father was taking notes on a yellow legal pad.

"I shoplifted a CD player one day. It was a stupid thing to do. I got probation."

"So that's when you decided to leave, to take on the identity of Sadie Sinclair?"

"I didn't steal her identity!" Sadie said, pounding the desk. "I told Bianca that already."

I looked at Sadie and wondered why she insisted on lying about that. Then it hit me. "She's right," I chimed in. "She didn't steal Sadie Mauvais Sinclair's identity. She only used her name." Then I explained that Sadie had made up a new Social Security number for herself. She hadn't stolen Sinclair's. She'd merely used the name after seeing it in the newspaper.

"How do you know what her Social Security number is?" Mr. Daniels asked me.

"Uh . . . uh . . ." I stammered. I really didn't think I wanted to reveal the story about how I looked at Sadie's school file. Call me crazy, but I had this idea that Mr. Daniels would feel obligated to notify some authorities. Some real ones. Not the Doug kind.

"I told her!" Sadie said, looking at me with gratitude in her eyes. "I told her one day."

Sadie explained the rest of the story in short order. Her mother, whose family was all gone now, had moved to California from Baltimore after graduating from St. John's. So Sadie had headed to her mother's home turf to get away from Dwayne and Angelica. But the Diabolical Duo were not good at the computer stuff. When their money-machine left, they decided they'd take a little trip, find her, and entice her back into the identity-theft ring. It was a cash cow, she said. By this time, Dwayne was writing counterfeit checks right and left using the fake corporation he'd set up and various other identities he'd managed to pilfer through Sadie's work.

"All I wanted to do was start over," Sadie said. "I wanted to get my high school diploma with the money from my mom and maybe go to college and find a job." She broke down again. Kerrie's dad told Kerrie to get a glass of water for Sadie.

Sadie had faked her age in order to pick up her high school career where she'd left off—right before she'd dropped out—as a sophomore.

By the time the story was over, Kerrie's dad was re-assuring Sadie that she would probably be all right. It was nearly midnight now and the party was winding down. I still had a lot of questions, but they would have to wait for another day. Right now, I just wanted to go home and get some shut-eye.

Doug drove me home, only missing my street once. He even managed to stay in his lane most of the time.

At my door, he gave me the kind of heart-stopping good-bye kiss that a girl dreams about. He put his hands on either side of my face and drew me close and, well, you'll excuse me if I keep some things private. When my diaries are published and I'm famous, you'll know all.

Until then, suffice it to say that I was in a kind of dreamy mood when I went to bed that night.

Oh, and did I mention? Doug asked me to the Mistletoe Dance.

Epilogue

Sadie, or Sarah as we came to know her, did okay. Kerrie's dad managed to cut a deal for her. She wasn't even charged with anything as long as she spilled her guts about Dwayne and Angelica, both of whom were extradited to California. ("Extradited," by the way, means that Maryland sent the pair back to their home state for prosecution. It's one of the many legal and criminal justice terms I am learning as I prepare for my new career.)

The nuns at St. John's kept Sadie on but adjusted her schedule to suit her age. She left our lowly sophomore class and resumed school as a senior, taking a few lower-level classes the rest of the year to make up for what she'd missed when she'd dropped out of school.

The condo that Sadie had stayed in belonged to one of Dwayne and Angelica's victims, who she knew was a convicted criminal already sent to prison.

Even though Sadie was "borrowing" the condo, she had still paid the rent. And by California standards, the rent didn't seem out of line. She never bothered to buy furniture because she used all her money for school and food—just the basics. The insurance she'd received from her mother was a fifty-thousand dollar policy. Mr. Daniels insisted she bank what was left for college.

Kerrie's parents took Sadie under their wing, which was a delight for Kerrie, who'd always wanted a sister. (It didn't take long, though, before Kerrie realized siblings are as much a bother as a boon. But that's another story.)

Sadie would stay with the Daniels the remainder of the school year, applying to colleges and working part-time in one of Mr. Daniels's client's businesses so she could make some extra money. She insisted on paying him for his legal help.

Because of her new schedule, I didn't see Sadie much over the next month when all this stuff was sorted out. But whenever I did, she gave me a big smile, which went a long way toward making me feel better about the whole mess. I had a nagging sense that I hadn't exactly handled it superbly.

I guess the moral of the story is a pretty simple one. It's easy to gossip and raise your eyebrows about the tribulations of others. It's far harder to roll up your sleeves and actually help out.

Hoping for the best but thinking the worst, we all like to snicker and guess when a friend looks headed for trouble. It would be better, though, to offer to solve those problems.

Such was the case with Sadie. I had known she had problems. And I'd wanted to think she was on the road out of whatever mess she was in. But at times I had thought the worst deep down—that she was into drugs or even prostitution.

In reality, she was running away from people who had exploited her. If I had been as tenacious in making her talk about it as I was in digging into her past, maybe she would have felt like she had a place to run to.

You see, I could have solved the Sadie mystery by being a little more insistent at the outset. From the way Sadie gave it all up in the Daniels's study that night, I don't think it would have taken much to get her to tell her story to us if we had persisted. Instead, we played Private Eye, which was risky, especially when the only "heat" you're packing is of the sugar-coated variety.

So it's less like a moral and more like an etiquette lesson. That is, it is preferable to ask one's friends directly if they have a problem rather than resorting to spying on, and speculating about, them. Sometimes the more direct approach is the best.

Speaking of best, this all ended well for me, too. Doug and I are seeing each other. When I'm not at school, out with Kerrie or Sadie, or out with Doug, I'm helping my mom sew that green velvet dress for the Misteltoe Dance.

Trust me, it's going to be a knock-out. The flapper costume will look like rags in comparison.